"WHAT'S WRONG WITH YOUR BROTHER?"

That's the first thing Noni was asked when she tried to make friends with pretty, popular Denise Baxly.

"Tell me, Noni," Denise said. "Your brother, Kip. Doesn't he go to school?" She waited a moment, then added, "He looks . . . well, a little weird. Is something wrong with him, or what?"

"No," Noni replied. "He doesn't go to school right now. He is *not* weird. My brother is special."

SIGNET Books You'll Enjoy

My Brother Is SPECIAL

by

Maureen Crane Wartski

A SIGNET BOOK

NEW AMERICAN LIBRARY

TIMES MIRROR

PUBLISHER'S NOTE

This novel is a work of fiction. Names, characters, places, and incidents are either the product of the author's imagination or are used fictitiously, and any resemblance to actual persons, living or dead, events, or locales is entirely coincidental.

 SIGNET TRADEMARK REG. U.S. PAT. OFF. AND FOREIGN COUNTRIES REGISTERED TRADEMARK—MARCA REGISTRADA
HECHO EN CHICAGO, U.S.A.

SIGNET, SIGNET CLASSICS, MENTOR, PLUME, MERIDIAN AND NAL BOOKS *are published by The New American Library, Inc., 1633 Broadway, New York, New York 10019*

FIRST SIGNET PRINTING, JANUARY, 1981

1 2 3 4 5 6 7 8 9

PRINTED IN THE UNITED STATES OF AMERICA

For my mother . . .
and for Debbie

ish, garbled because she ated so much to

1

Saturday morning Noni woke up knowing she was going to beat Denise Baxly in the 100-yard dash.

All night she had dreamed of racing, of feet flying over the track at Conan Junior High. The interscholastic track meet with Franklin was to be held today. Though it would be hard besting Franklin's athletes, Noni knew that an even tougher contest was facing her. As Denise had pointed out yesterday in her snotty way, she, Denise, was captain of the junior high girls' track team, while this was Noni Harlow's first track meet, ever!

The Harlows had moved to Conan, Massachusetts, a few months back. The school Noni had gone to in Lincoln hadn't gone in for track. You had to wait till high school for that, and Noni was just in the eighth grade. Noni was homesick for California, where she had lived all her life before Dad's company had relocated him to the East Coast. She had hated Lincoln. They had arrived there in November, and the dreary gray of the city streets and buildings made Noni want to cry. She often *did* cry during her first weeks in Lincoln, cooped up with her nearly nine-year-old brother, Kip, in Aunt Mary's apartment.

1

Aunt Mary was Mom's older sister. She had kindly offered the extra rooms in her apartment till they could "get settled," and then she proceeded to boss them all around. It was an awful time.

Nor did it get better. Noni hated the big, impersonal junior high to which she had been assigned, and later, the large, blank-walled apartment Dad found for the family, but it was Kip who suffered most. Kip just couldn't understand why they had left California, and why they couldn't go back. He loathed the special program in which he had been enrolled at Dad's and Aunt Mary's insistence. He whined, caught colds, and threw tantrums through the long, dreary winter, making life miserable for everyone.

Then, in January, Dad had been transferred to a branch office in Conan. Dad didn't enjoy the transfer, saying it was really a demotion and that Conan was a dead-end town. Noni had been delighted.

Conan was a pretty place. It had a modern junior high and a great new gym. It was bordered on one side by a strip of beach and the Atlantic Ocean. There was even a shuttle bus that came down Main Street every hour, taking you to shop in nearby Haymarket or to the beach. The people seemed friendly, and Noni's spirits rose. Maybe she would like Conan as much as she had liked California.

Then, she had met Denise Baxly. Denise lived on Noni's street, Pleasant Street, four doors down. The Baxly home was the prettiest and by far the largest on the block. Before she knew her very well, Noni had wanted to become friends with Denise, who went to school with her, and was popular and pretty and smart. Noni was too shy, though, to say anything to Denise, until she learned that Denise was captain of the track team. This delighted Noni. Now they had something in common, something to share.

Noni always felt a little sick when she remembered her first talk with Denise. She had begun it so eagerly, on the bus, coming home from school one afternoon. "I hear you're captain of the girls' track team," she had said, and Denise nodded, gray eyes questioning. "I love to run too," innocent Noni hurried on. "I'm pretty fast . . ."

Before Denise could respond, one of Denise's friends, Marcie, giggled. "Watch it, Denise—if Noni's as swift as she claims, she may break your records!"

Denise's eyes had clouded over, and she had changed the subject. "Tell me, Noni," she said. "Your brother, Kip. Doesn't he go to school?" She waited a moment, then added, "He looks . . . well, a little weird. Is something wrong with him, or what?"

Hurt, Noni had stammered that Kip didn't go to school right now. Mom hadn't been able to place him in the special school at Haymarket. But while she was talking, the tall blond Denise turned her back, ignoring her. As if Noni didn't even exist!

"Noni!"

Kip's cry broke into Noni's thoughts. "Noni!" he called again, and she heard footsteps hurrying to her bedroom door. In a moment Kip poked a tear-stained face through the doorway. "Noni . . . come," he said. "L'il Bird . . . sick!"

L'il Bird was Kip's pet canary and lived in a cage in Kip's room. "What's wrong with L'il

Bird?" Noni asked Kip, but he just stood there, looking at her.

From downstairs, Mom called, "Noni? See what Kip wants!"

"Show me," Noni said resignedly. Kip took her hand and led her down the hall to his room. His hand was shaking, and Noni saw why. The little canary lay dead, a crumpled heap, at the bottom of its cage. Noni wondered how she was going to explain this.

It was never easy explaining things to Kip. Looking at him now, Noni remembered how Mom had cried when she had told Noni about Kip's problems. "Kip wasn't born like other children. God made him different. His body will grow, but his mind will stay little." She had said all this as if repeating a lesson she hadn't wanted to learn. "He'll always be . . . innocent."

And often, difficult. Kip held Noni's hand, looked up at her with pleading brown eyes. Kip had brown eyes like mom, and Dad's curly brown-gold hair. Noni had the coloring herself, except that Kip's round softness was, in her, all angles and bones and long, awkward legs—awkward, that is, except when she was running. Recently, her nose had grown sharp too, so that when Denise started calling her "the Running Nose," it had stuck.

"Kip, L'il Bird's . . . well, he went to God," she began.

"No!" he shrilled. He flung Noni's hand away and started working himself into a tantrum. Mom appeared in the doorway and Kip ran to her, burrowing his face into her skirt, howling. Over Kip's head, Mom's eyes met Noni's.

"It's getting late," Mom said, "Go eat, honey. Breakfast is on the table."

Noni left quickly. Kip's howls followed her as she got dressed and went downstairs to eat. The confidence she had felt earlier this morning was trickling away. She tried to get it back by quoting Mrs. Balkans, the junior high girls' bird-thin, red-headed coach. "I'm a winner," Noni told herself, unconsciously mimicking Mrs. Balkans' peppery way of talking. "I'll beat that Baxly . . ."

Baxly. Denise asking about Kip's "weirdness" as if it were something shameful. Denise cold-shouldering Noni in the lunchroom, ignoring her after track practice, excluding her from conversations with her friends. Denise appearing so sugary sweet and smart in front of people she wanted to impress . . . so snotty to Noni! "You'll never beat me in the 100-yard dash, Noni. I'm a lot faster, don't you know that?"

Noni pushed her breakfast away. The sad part was that at one time she had thought she could be Denise's friend.

"Noni?" Mom's voice came from upstairs. She sounded harried. "You'd best have Dad drive you to school!" Kip began wailing and Noni could hear the thuds he made as he kicked the floor. Her heart sank.

"You're coming, aren't you? My first meet. You said you'd come!"

Kip's howls rose so Noni could only catch fragments of Mom's reply. "Come if we can . . . calm Kip down . . . medication Dr. Farrell gave us . . ."

Noni turned away bitterly. Why did Kip have to spoil it all?

The back door banged, and Dad came in,

frowning against the glare of the outside sun. "All ready?" he began, and then his frown deepened. "What's happening here?"

Noni explained, and her bitterness grew stronger as she saw her father's shoulders slump. Dad was a tall man, but he hunched over so that he looked shorter. "I'll drive you to school," he said, not looking at her but up the stairs to where Kip sobbed and wailed.

"I'll get my stuff," Noni muttered, and Dad nodded absently, as if he had heard her but didn't really care very much. Noni thought about that as she got her things and followed Dad to the garage. Dad had changed so much. He either looked tired, or he exploded over small, silly things. It wasn't just Dad, either. Lately, Mom spoke, moved, even smiled with a helplessness in her eyes. Noni knew she herself had become more shy, quieter, like a snail slowly withdrawing into its shell.

It hadn't always been this way—only since Kip had been diagnosed back in California: moderately retarded, trainable.

Noni glanced at Dad, driving with the frown between his eyebrows. *Moderately retarded, trainable*—easy, terrible words that had ripped the family apart.

They were at the junior high. "Here we are," Dad said. "Good luck, Noni." He waited for her to open the door and get out.

Noni started to open the door, then glanced at the athletic field where kids from Conan and Franklin were warming up. Franklin buses, bright with streamers, stood in the school parking lot. Laughter and shouting and the sound of the band tuning up made excitement bubble into her throat.

She grabbed Dad's hand. He looked surprised as she cried, "Dad, please come to watch me run? Please?"

For a moment he stared, then his eyes turned angry. Noni thought he was mad at her, but instead he said, "You bet we'll come. He won't spoil this day for you!"

Noni knew he was mad at Kip. She sensed how mad by the way Dad's tires squealed as he drove away. Her brief excitement faded.

She tried to get it back, walking across to where her team was doing warm-up exercises. Across the way, Conan Junior High's boys were gathered around their coach, Mr. Crusoe. From the look on Mr. Crusoe's face, he was talking about winning. Mrs. Balkans seemed to be talking about winning too, but when Noni came up to the knot of girls gathered around the small, redheaded coach, Mrs. Balkans was saying, "So, as you run today, I want you to give thanks for your fine, strong bodies and healthy minds . . . such as they are."

There was a chorus of giggled. "What's she talking about?" Noni whispered to the girl next to her, Brenda. Before Brenda could answer, another girl turned—a tall, blond girl with cool gray eyes. Denise Baxly.

"Mrs. Balkans is talking about a special track meet, Noni," she said very loudly. "Too bad you came late and missed it all."

Ignoring Denise, Noni looked questioningly at her coach. "We were discussing the Special Olympics, Noni, designed for unfortunate children who are handicapped, retarded. Kids who can't compete like you, in regular sports. I was pointing out how grateful you should be." Mrs. Balkans paused. "Now let's talk about what we're all here for today. Let me hear it, girls."

Unfortunate children . . . handicapped . . . retarded. Noni felt a part of her grow tense, hard. Mrs. Balkans spoke of them as if they were creatures from another planet!

"What are we here for, ladies?" Mrs. Balkans was demanding.

"To WIN!" they screamed. Noni yelled loudest of all. She wanted to believe that winning could block out everything else.

The team broke up and began warm-ups again. Denise fell in step beside Noni. "Noni, you know Red Balkans didn't mean anything personal just now, don't you?"

"I don't know what you mean."

"You do too. Too bad there's no local meet in Conan . . . for your brother, I mean," Denise insisted.

"Maybe he'd break Neill Oliver's record for the 400!" Marcie giggled. Denise smiled, and Noni felt hot rage. Neill was the school's top athlete, and Denise's boyfriend. How dare Denise and her creepy pals laugh at Kip? I'll show you, Noni thought. Wait!

She had to wait a long while. The boys' teams ran their main events first—the 100-yard dash, the 294 relay. When Neill won the first hands down and was anchorman in the second, Noni clapped as hard as anyone else. She admired Neill's speed, his control. It made her think of her own. Control and concentration, she reminded herself. Don't get angry. Concentrate on running . . .

Finally, it was her event. After the boys' relay,

the girls' obstacle race, and the jumps, the girls' 100-yard dash was announced. Noni, Denise, and Brenda took their places at the starting line beside three Franklin challengers.

For the past fifteen minutes, Noni had been glancing at the bleachers that ringed the field. She had seen Denise's parents there—Denise's college professor father, her elegant mother, but no Harlows . . . not one! Now, as she stood at the starting line, she realized that her parents had finally arrived. They were walking toward the stands, with Kip between them. He seemed subdued, and walked slowly. Mom had probably given him the tranquilizer Dr. Farrell had prescribed for his "difficult" times. Hurry! Noni wanted to shout at them as Denise gave her a cool, superior smile.

"Good luck, Noni." Her gray eyes added, You'll need it!

"On your MARK . . ."

Concentration, Noni thought. She leaned forward, her weight on her two hands and left knee. She pushed the ball of her left foot flat against the front block, loosening up the right leg and straightening her elbows.

"Get SET . . ."

She moved her weight forward just a little, hips lifting so they were slightly higher than her shoulders. She focused her eyes on a point a few feet ahead of her, drew a deep breath.

"GO!" The pistol cracked.

Noni went. For a second she felt excitement, fear, tightness, and then it was gone. Her body, arms, shoulders, legs were moving together with her breath, her heartbeat. She forgot Denise, Kip, even herself. She was running . . . a blur of speed, unthinking . . .

"No-neee!" Her own name filled her ears with a burst of sound as she hit the tape. She glanced over her shoulder. Behind her, face taut with effort, was Denise Baxly.

I won, she thought. I *won!*

Things became confused. Mrs. Balkans hugged her. Girls from her track team swarmed over her. Even Marcie grudgingly congratulated her on speed. Denise made some remark about "beginner's luck" but not even Denise could spoil this moment. Noni's chest felt squeezed with joy, triumph, elation. She felt so alive she knew she could easily jump the moon.

When they pinned the "First" ribbon on her jersey, her thoughts were of her folks. Now they would be glad they had come! Even though she was entered in the girls' 294-yard relay, just an event away, she ran to where her family was sitting. Mom gave Noni a big hug and Dad was really smiling for the first time in a while. "You ran so fast we thought you were flying," he teased.

Then Kip spoke up. "Ribbon. I want ribbon!"

Dad's smile didn't disappear, but the frown slid over it, a cloud over the sun. "No, Son. That's Noni's. She gets to wear it." Kip's face began to screw up and Dad's voice sharpened. "Don't start, or I take you home!"

Mom's face changed. "Jim—please!"

"Dina, what's the use of giving him everything he wants? It's your fault. You spoil him. He can't be lived with."

Were her folks going to hassle over Kip right here and now? With everyone, including the

Baxlys, listening? Noni wanted to die from embarrassment. She jerked the ribbon off her jersey. "Here—here!" She handed the ribbon to Kip. "Have it!"

Her first ribbon. She felt a spurt of resentment. It wasn't fair!

She stormed out of the stands, walked back to the field. Why did he have to come anyway? Why didn't he stay home, the brat? Behind her, she thought she heard Kip call her name, but she didn't bother to turn around. Let Mom baby him and take care of him!

She walked back to her team, tried to concentrate on what Mrs. Balkans was saying. "Now, Denise, you're anchorperson, so you know what you have to do. Noni, you're very fast. Make sure you give us a lead . . . you're first. Now, loosen up."

Noni began to turn away, then stopped. A little distance away from the grandstand Kip was standing, turning this way and that, bewildered by the crowd and the noise and disoriented because of his medication. He was looking for her. He had evidently followed her off the stands to give her back her blue ribbon, because he was holding it out in a dazed way.

He began to shamble off in the wrong direction. She started to move toward him, but slowly. She was still mad at him. So what if Dad had forced him to give back the ribbon, she still hated the way he had acted. She wasn't going to forget his grabbiness right away. Then she saw the children . . .

There were three of them, two girls and a boy. They were younger than Kip, but they were taller than he was, stronger. They were talking to him—

no, laughing at him. Noni saw one of the little girls grab at the ribbon in Kip's hand.

"Hey!" Noni shouted and began to run as Kip mouthed the word, "Mine!"

"How could *you* win anything?" the boy taunted. He gave Kip a push, knocking him backward. Still Kip hung on to the ribbon. Noni was almost there when she saw one of the girls lean over—and spit. The spittle landed on Kip's cheek, and at the same moment the boy grabbed the ribbon, danced off with it.

"Hey—you kids! You little creeps, you come back here!" Noni hollered. They saw her, turned, and scattered into the crowd, the boy dropping the ribbon as he ran. Noni picked it out of the dust, fury making her hands shake. Why? she kept thinking. They didn't even want it . . .

She turned back to where Kip was sitting in the dirt. He wasn't even crying, nor was he moving, he was just sitting. And then she saw his eyes, his sad, bewildered, longing eyes.

Suddenly it seemed to Noni that she was seeing her brother for the first time ever. He *knew* he would never have a "First" ribbon. He knew he would never be a winner. He would never hear the crowd shout his name or feel the burning joy of winning.

"Kippy—" she whispered.

He got up, dusty and scared now. "Ma-a," she heard him bleat as he hurried away toward where her parents sat. People turned to stare, and Noni felt her heart crack.

It was then she remembered what Mrs. Balkans had said about the Special Olympics.

2

Noni wondered why people avoided looking at her directly when they used the words "handicapped" and "retarded." Mrs. Balkans didn't meet her eyes when she went to see the coach Monday right after school.

Noni had wanted to see Mrs. Balkans after the meet on Saturday, but she hadn't been able to get the coach alone. Mrs. Balkans, like everyone else, had been crowding around Denise, congratulating her on winning so many firsts for Conan. Noni herself hadn't been able to run at all after what happened to Kip. Her timing was off, and as Denise pointed out, she had nearly lost the relay for Conan by getting a slow start.

Now Mrs. Balkans said, "The Special Olympics? Why, sure. I have some pamphlets in my office. Your brother, Kip, is a . . . a special child, then?" Noni nodded, stiffening at the pitying tone. "Does he go to the school of the—uh-retarded at Haymarket?"

"Not right now," Noni admitted. "There's a waiting list and everything. But he was in school in California and . . . and in Lincoln."

"It must have been hard for you to leave California," Mrs. Balkans probed. "What happened in

Lincoln? Did your brother like the school he went to there?"

"For a while." Noni didn't want to think about the program Kip had gone to in Lincoln. He had loved going to school in California, where he had learned to tie his own shoes, button buttons, go to the bathroom alone, be polite to people. But the program in Lincoln had been a disaster. Both Aunt Mary and Dad had been so enthusiastic about the program and about what Kip could achieve if he only tried. Unfortunately, all the kids in the program had been smarter than Kip, and he had become frustrated and angry, lashing out at home and throwing tantrums. Mom had wanted to take him out of the program, but Dad had insisted that his son was no quitter. He had insisted right up to that awful day when Kip ran away from school. No one could find him. He had been lost for hours, and finally the police had found him in an alleyway, cowering, lost, terrified, crying . . .

No, Noni didn't like to think of that, nor of the fight Dad and Mom had had while Kip was still lost, each blaming the other for what had happened. Even worse was Aunt Mary's reaction: "Dina," she had said to Mom, "I've told you that that child is better off in an institution!" That part really made Noni want to barf.

"About the Special Olympics, Mrs. Balkans," she prodded.

"It'll take a while to hunt the pamphlets up. Let's look for them together." Noni had to admit that her coach's office was a mess. Mrs. Balkans' desk was buried under piles of papers. Finally, she pulled out a handful of pamphlets.

"Here," she said. "Here we are. Special Olym-

pics, open to all mentally retarted children and
adults over the age of eight—" She began to hand
the booklets to Noni, then stopped. "Did you
know there's going to be a local meet in Haymarket a few weeks from now?"

"A local meet?" Noni didn't understand.

Mrs. Balkans explained that kids competed first
on a local level, then regionally, then went on to
state and national levels. "Kids who win go on to
international meets," she finished.

"International?" Noni could see Kip carrying
an Olympic torch high as he zoomed around a
track in Paris, Tokyo, Rome . . .

"The director of the Haymarket meet is a friend
of mine, Jean McKenna. She could tell you more
about this. She sent me these pamphlets to find
out if I could help, but—" Mrs. Balkans shrugged
ruefully. "No time. Here's her address if you want
to contact her for more information."

Noni murmured thanks while looking at a sil-
houetted photo of a young boy bounding up
against the sky. This could be Kip!

She hurried out of the office and went outside to
sit on the school steps. She couldn't wait to read
what was in the booklets. Before reading the text,
she scanned the photos: kids in wheelchairs,
braces, who were riding or running in special
races! Kids pole-vaulting. Kids playing basketball.
Kids being awarded medals, smiling, proud kids.

They're winners, Noni thought.

She began to read. The Special Olympics had
begun in 1963. Since then, almost 200,000 volunteers had brought skills and pride to kids and
adults like Kip who hadn't thought they could
join sports. More than 15,000 games and meets
and training programs throughout the country

kept the Special Olympics going year round. Countries like Australia, France, Japan, and others made it possible for kids to say together at Special Olympics meets: "Let me win, but if I cannot win, let me be brave in the attempt . . ."

Noni got choked up when she read that. Kip could do this, she thought. People were grouped by ability level, not age. Every step forward was cheered, and the retarded gained confidence in themselves while they became stronger physically.

"Hey, Noni!" Noni glanced up, saw Neill Oliver standing at the bottom of the school steps looking up at her.

"Studying?" Neill asked.

Noni hugged the booklets close to her. She didn't want anyone to know about them, especially not Neill, who might tell Denise Baxly!

"Not really," she said. "Just reading."

Neill hadn't spoken more than fifteen words to her before today, but now he walked up the steps and sat down beside her. His eyes were very blue under his fair hair.

"Bet a test wouldn't bother you. You're probably as fast in your head as you are on your feet." He smiled, and his teeth glinted with his braces. "Someday I'll race you, and you'll probably beat me."

"I wish!" Noni laughed, then saw his attention drift away. Denise was coming out of the school building, talking to Mrs. Balkans. Of course, Neill was only waiting for Denise. Noni got up quickly, dropping some booklets in her hurry. She didn't want to talk to Denise right now!

Neill helped her pick up the booklets, and she saw him glance at one as he handed it to her.

"See you," she muttered, hurrying away.

Would Neill mention the booklet to Denise? Quit worrying what other people will do, Noni told herself sternly. She pulled her mind back to thinking about the Special Olympics. She couldn't wait to get home and hand the booklets to Mom and Dad and tell them how Kip could be a winner.

She was impatient waiting for the bus to come and pick her up so she could get home. But as she walked through the back door of her house, she realized Mom had company. There were voices coming from the living room. Who? Noni wondered. Since moving to Conan, her mother had made no effort to make friends.

"We're in here, Noni!" Mom called. Noni poked her head into the living room and was surprised to see Mrs. Baxly, of all people.

Mrs. Baxly looked like an older version of Denise, blond, good-looking, elegant even in a shirt and a pair of jeans.

"Hi, Noni. That was a fine race you ran yesterday. I *told* Denise she had underestimated your speed!" Noni mumbled her thanks, and Mrs. Baxly continued, "I'm here on a mission today, trying to convince your mother to join our RES-CAB committee. That stands for 'Restore Ecology, Save Conan's Animals and Birds.'" She paused. "I chair the committee. We need all the help we can get."

Noni glanced at Mom, who was looking uncertain. "I don't know . . ." she began.

"Oh, nonsense." Mrs. Baxly even sounded like Denise, sure of herself, bound to get her own way. "All you need to do, Dina, is call people on the phone, address some envelopes. You've lived in Conan long enough, I'm sure, to realize that pollution is a reality for us. Look at the oil that got dumped into our ocean when that oil tanker ran aground off our coast!"

Mom looked blank, but Noni remembered what Mr. Turello, her science teacher, had said. "Oil is a killer, a poison in the water. It poisons fish, seals, whales . . . fouls the feathers of water birds. The birds try to preen, ingest the oil, and die."

"The committee had a cleanup at Conan beach at the time the tanker ran aground," Mrs. Baxly said. "We saved many gulls and murres. The work goes on. There's a meeting at my home tomorrow."

Mom looked flushed. "I can't come. I have my son at home."

"Oh, I forgot. He doesn't go to school, does he?" Mrs. Baxly frowned. "It's at my house, so why not bring him? He *can* play alone?"

She asked the question so smoothly that the words left a sting that was not quite a sting. Noni saw her mother hesitate, not quite knowing how to answer, and blurted, "My brother is really very human, Mrs. Baxly!"

Color stained Mrs. Baxly's cheeks, and she looked embarrassed and angry. Noni was surprised that she had had the guts to speak up like that. She waited for Denise's mother to shout her down, but Mrs. Baxly ignored Noni and said, "See you tomorrow, Dina."

When she had gone, Mom turned to Noni. "That wasn't too polite," she said.

"Well, neither was she! I don't like her. Neither does Kip. I bet he ran off to his room the second she got here. She's gross."

"Hardly," Mom said bitterly. "She's polished,

educated, wealthy, and chairs every organization in Conan. She made a point of telling me that she had a friend on the board of directors at the special school in Haymarket."

Here was the opening Noni needed to talk about the Haymarket meet! She started to hold out the pamphlets, when the phone began to ring. Mom picked up the receiver and a crisp voice said, "Dina? This is Mary."

Aunt Mary! Noni groaned inwardly. Bossy Aunt Mary! Now she wouldn't be able to talk to her mother for quite a while. Aunt Mary's calls always upset Mom for hours, because she always nagged Mom to do something about "that child."

Noni went upstairs and started toward her room. Then, changing her mind, she crossed the hall to peer into Kip's room. He was sitting on the floor, pushing a truck around and around. Noni guessed that he had been there since Mrs. Baxly's arrival. Sometimes it was uncanny just how Kip knew who was a friend and who wasn't.

"Hiya," Kip said, grinning at Noni. "Hi, Noni."

"Hi, Kippo." She went in and sat down on his bed, looking him over critically the way Mrs. Balkans assessed her track team. Kip was small, and he was also somewhat pudgy. Not surprising, Noni thought. Kip didn't get much exercise. Back in California, Dad had often taken his son into the backyard to throw a ball or play tag. Kip had been clumsy, though, and hadn't followed instructions. This had frustrated both of them. Now Dad didn't take Kip out to play with him anymore.

I should have done something with him, Noni thought remorsefully, chewing her lip. It's going to take a while to get him into shape. And that Haymarket meet isn't that far away . . .

Sudden fear came to her. Would there be enough time to train Kip to compete? There *had* to be time! She would start now, this minute!

"Let's go outside, Kip," she said.

Kip considered her, then his truck. "No."

"Aw, come on. It's a nice day. Mrs. Baxly's gone."

Kip jutted his jaw stubbornly. "Kip plays here."

"Kip—" But Noni knew it was hopeless. Kip had plenty of the Harlow stubborn streak. How was she going to get Kip to train? Maybe that lady in Haymarket, Mrs. McKenna, could give her some ideas. And, of course, Dad and Mom would know what to do.

She looked around Kip's room, saw a ball. "How about if we throw a ball to each other?" she suggested.

"Okay." Kip got up and got the ball. "Here!" he said. "Not outside!"

"Suit yourself." He was not badly coordinated, Noni thought. The booklets said that he would compete with kids of his own ability. There *was* a good chance. She tossed the ball gently to Kip, saw him struggle to catch it. He dropped it the first two times, started to get frustrated, then caught the ball. Noni praised him, thinking, he needs so much work! What events could I train him for? The softball throw? The 50-yard dash?

Crash!

Kip threw the ball back at her, catching her off balance. It smashed through the window. Glass flew all over the room.

"What's going on? What's happening?" Mom shouted from downstairs. Kip stuck his thumb in his mouth, his dark eyes telling Noni that was the end of *his* fun and games.

"Nothing, Mom!" Noni yelled. "The window—"

"A window! You call that nothing?" Mom's voice had a gritty edge to it. She came up the stairs, glaring at Noni. "In Kip's room, too. He'll catch a cold again, for heaven's sake! Go get a broom right now and sweep this up, Noni. You're the most irresponsible child . . ."

Noni wanted to talk back, but she didn't. That was how Mom always talked after a call from Aunt Mary. Aunt Mary had probably talked and talked about how bad it was for Kip not to be in some learning situation. She always fussed and bossed. Mom could never tell Aunt Mary to go hang her advice in her ear, so instead she yelled at Noni.

"You only think about yourself!" Mom was scolding. Noni bit her lip and felt angry tears lump into her throat. Mom went into her own room and slammed the door, hard.

Kip whimpered. He didn't like the moods that were building up. Noni glared at him. "You're going to be a winner," she snapped at him, "even if it kills me. Don't touch the glass!" It was going to be tough, trying to find the proper time to tell her folks about the Special Olympics, with Mom in a mood like this!

3

SUPPER WAS LATE that evening, and that put Mom in an even worse mood. It was late because Dad got home late from work, his shoulders more hunched than usual, his lips pressed tight together. He barely patted Kip's head in greeting, and he didn't ask how Noni's day at school had gone. As they grouped around the dining room table, Noni tried to make things better.

"Hard day?" she asked Dad.

Mom fielded that one. "There seems to be no other kind," she said, her voice flat and bitter. Dad looked at her, but said nothing. Mom continued, "Just once, I'd like to have one good, happy day without anything going wrong. Just once."

"And if there ever came such a day, you'd ruin it by worrying," Dad muttered.

"Thank you," Mom said so coldly that Noni ducked her head and ate without looking, without tasting the cottony food. Across from her, Kip stared at his folks with sad eyes. He knew things weren't right. "Mary called me, today, on the phone," Mom continued. "She nagged me about Kip, as usual."

Dad let his breath out in an I-get-it sigh. "Why don't you tell your bossy sister off?" he demanded. "Or else do something positive about Kip."

Mom squared her shoulders. "I certainly see *you* being brave and positive," she shrilled. "How about work, Jim? Do you stand up to your boss? Did you stand up when your home office moved you from California to Lincoln, Massachusetts, forcing us to leave a home we all loved?"

"Stop talking about that!" Dad exploded. "That's all in the past. I'm talking about things that can be changed *now!* And I'm saying that you've been holding Kip back. You don't even *call* that school in Haymarket to see if they can take him!"

They glared at each other in the anger that had become so much a part of the family. And the pain . . . for Mom's eyes were sparkling with tears. Noni wanted to say something, but there was a lump in her throat that stopped her. Then Dad bowed his head.

"Sorry, Dina," he muttered.

Mom wiped her eyes, and Noni let her breath out gratefully. The storm was over—for now. Dad turned to her. "Now, Noni. How was your day?"

Should she bring it up now? With Kip sitting here? Why not! "I heard something really interesting today," she began.

But Mom broke in, talking about Mrs. Baxly's visit. Dad began to frown again. "There you go again, Dina! Why not get friendly with Alice Baxly? She could help Kip get into Haymarket. I just don't understand the way you think."

They would start hassling again at any second, so Noni said louder, "I know a way to help Kip!"

They turned to look at her, and Dad frowned. "I heard you broke a window in Kip's room."

"Because I was trying to help him train . . . for the Special Olympics!" The words came out in a rush, garbled because she wanted so much to get them out, get them said. "They're games for kids like Kip. Retarded kids."

Mom said nothing. No "Oh, really?" No interest. Nothing!

Dad said, "I've heard about the Special Olympics. I know about the program."

Noni was too excited to hear the way Dad said that. She jumped from her seat, raced upstairs to her room to get the booklets. On her way down she nearly slipped and fell headfirst down the stairs.

"Look!" she cried. "Look at the kids!" She thrust the booklets in front of Mom. "Here's the name of the woman who's directing the meet at Haymarket. Jean McKenna. You could call her. Kip could win!"

"Win?" Kip picked up that word.

"Yes, Kippo!" Noni began happily, when Mom said sharply, "Kip, honey, wash your hands and go watch TV for a minute, okay?" She waited till he had gone and then turned to Noni.

"Noni, both your father and I know about the Special Olympics. The director of the school in Haymarket told us that Kip could compete if he wished, this spring, even though he isn't a member of the school."

"But then, why—" Noni was so surprised she could hardly speak. "Don't you want Kip to enter the meet?"

Mom shook her head. "No," she said.

For a second, Noni stared. "But—but look at them!" She pointed to the beaming kids in the booklets, the proud winners with the medals around their necks. "Kip could be proud—like that!"

"What happens if he doesn't succeed?" Dad asked. "I wanted Kip to enter the games when I first heard about them. But your mother wouldn't hear of it. We talked it over, and I have to admit she has a point. Kip shouldn't be forced into a situation where he would have to compete with other kids." As if to himself, he added, "There was that bad, bad scene in Lincoln. Hiding like an animal in an alleyway. My son!"

Noni couldn't say a word.

"Noni, I know you mean well. I know you do this because you love Kip, but Kip mightn't be able to handle losing."

"You keep saying that as if you think he can't win!" Noni cried. She remembered Kip holding her blue ribbon in his small hands. "Don't you want him to win?"

"Kip doesn't remember instructions. Besides, kids need to be well trained for weeks and weeks before they can compete in the special games. Something like thirty hours of training over a period of several months—" Mom's voice quivered suddenly. "I won't allow him to be tormented as he was the day those kids took that blue ribbon away from him . . ."

"You saw it?" Noni asked, bewildered.

"That, and a lot more. Noni, darling, every day when you go to school do you know that Kip climbs up on the couch in the living room and watches till you're out of sight? He watches the younger kids come by to wait for their bus, and I know he longs to go with them. One time he even got his coat and ran outside, and they—"

"Dina," Dad said suddenly, "don't do this!"

"They laughed at him and pushed him and called him a retard," Mom said, her voice jerky but her eyes dry. "He's been hurt so much for something that's not this fault. I will not let him be hurt again."

Noni wished she could get her hands on those kids. Her fingers itched to slap, punch, push.

"But if he *won*!" she insisted.

"I won't allow it," Mom said. "No local meets. No regionals. No state games with parties and dances and celebrities coming to pity my son and call him retarded. I won't have it."

Dad went over to Mom and put his arms around her. Noni felt shut out—totally excluded, even from their grief. She hadn't known all that about Kip. She had known kids picked on him— she had whipped a few, back in California, for doing just that. But once they got to know Kip, people had accepted him.

"Try to understand," Dad said as she left the room, "it's for Kip's own good." But as Noni climbed the stairs to her room she wondered. Was it? Was it really?

Was it for Kip's good to give up? Or did he need someone to fight for him? Me, she thought, I'm all that's left. They've given up, but I'd fight for him. The question was, How?

Noni turned the booklets around in her hands, as if they could give her an answer. Perhaps if she called Mrs. Jean McKenna, Mrs. McKenna might give her some ideas. Maybe Mrs. McKenna would know how to change her parents' minds.

I'll call her tomorrow, Noni thought. I'll call her from school. I'll call her during third period—that's study. The prospect of phoning a perfect stranger chilled her for a second, but not so much as the next question hovering in the back of her mind.

Supposing Mrs. McKenna told her to forget about entering Kip in the Special Olympics meet?

Should she forget? Should she quit right now? Maybe Mom and Dad were right. There had to be things she didn't know about Kip. Anyway, who was to say that Kip would even *want* to enter the meet at Haymarket? What made her think the meet would make things any better for Kip, or solve anything for any of them?

"Should I forget about it? Maybe I should," she muttered into the silence.

The silence didn't answer, but suddenly into her mind came that moment of the total triumph, the joy, the elation, the jump-the-moon happiness Noni had felt when she won the 100-yard dash.

And Noni knew she had to give Kip that moment.

4

Noni sat in science with a headache and a queasy stomach, listening to Mr. Turello talk about pollution. To Mr. Turello, the tons of crude oil that poured from oil tankers into the sea was the world's greatest evil and problem. Noni had a problem that seemed a lot bigger. It made her want to throw up.

What was she going to say to Mrs. McKenna, now that the time was nearing? In a few moments the buzzer would go, study would begin. She could get a pass from the study aide, go down the hall and dial the number she had copied on a piece of paper last night. Now the paper was a greasy ball in her palm, and she was tempted to rip it up. She couldn't call Mrs. McKenna and say ... Oh, what was she going to say?

There was a silence in the classroom, and Noni realized that everyone was staring at someone. Not someone—her! Even Neill, sitting up front with Denise, had twisted around. "We're waiting, Noni," Mr. Turello said, deadly calm. "I asked a question."

Her face felt on fire as she shook her head. "I didn't hear the question," she mumbeld.

Mr. Turello said disgustedly, "We assumed as much. Denise?" Denise quickly gave the answer, and he added, "It's a pleasure to have someone who is *with* us and not out in left field!"

"Must run in the family." Had someone really said that? Noni whirled, and saw Marcie and Brenda sitting there. Marcie gave Noni a wide-eyed innocent stare. Who, me? Noni thought of oil flowing into the sea, the color of hate. She hated Marcie.

"Noni, I am over here, not behind you!" Mr. Turello scolded. Denise giggled.

The buzzer went!

Thankfully, Noni jumped up, dropping some of her books in her hurry to get away from them all. It wasn't till she was halfway to room 203 and study that she realized there was some truth in the old saying about the devil and the deep-blue sea. There was Mrs. McKenna, waiting to be called!

Maybe Mrs. McKenna wasn't home. The cowardly hope actually comforted Noni as, pass clutched tight in her hand, she dropped her dime into the coin slot and dialed. The phone began to ring.

One ring . . . two . . . three. Relief began to build up in Noni. She's not home. Well, I tried. Five, six . . . I'm going to hang up, Noni thought. This must mean that Kip's not meant to join the—

"Hello?" a voice said.

Caught up in the middle of her thought, Noni blurted, "Special Olympics? No . . . Mrs. McKenna?" The voice, sounding amused, said it was. "I'm calling for my little brother, Kip. About the meet." Noni was glad no one could see her face. "Mrs. Balkans said you were in charge of the Haymarket meet."

"Yes, I am." The voice was kind, and Noni felt her insides begin to unbunch. "Is your brother going to be one of our Olympians?"

Olympian. How nice that sounded! "I'd like to enter him," Noni said. "My name is Noni Harlow. My brother's Kip. He's nine—"

"Well," Mrs. McKenna hesitated, and Noni tensed again. "You see, there isn't really much time left. We require our athletes to have a certain amount of training to prepare them for this meet. Has your little brother been active in sports, or in a training program? The Special Olympics is the result of hours of work."

Noni had to say no. There was no program for Kip in Conan.

"How would your brother get ready for our meet?" Mrs. McKenna continued. "Perhaps you know some trained person willing to help you?"

"There's Mrs. Balkans—" Noni stopped, appalled. It had come out before she could stop herself!

"I know Joyce Balkans very well," Mrs. McKenna said. "If she feels that Kip could benefit by participating in our meet, that he's ready physically and emotionally, that's just fine with me. I'll gladly send you some forms. There's a Special Olympics entry form, a parents' release, and a medical form that you'll have to get back to me as soon as possible."

Medical form? Parents' release? Noni realized Mrs. McKenna was waiting for her home address. But she couldn't have those forms sent home, with Mom feeing the way she did!

"Please send the forms to . . . to Mrs. Balkans here at school," Noni said quickly. "We just moved and . . . anyway, I'd rather get them at school."

This was getting complicated. Mrs. McKenna must think Noni really weird! But she only said she would send the forms to Mrs. Balkins. "And good luck, Noni," she added, "to you and Kip."

Noni hung up, ready to pass out. Oh, wow, she thought.

How dumb could she get? Why did she have to go and give Mrs. Balkans' name to Jean Mc-Kenna? If Mrs. Balkans had been interested in training anybody, never mind Kip, wouldn't she have contacted Mrs. McKenna personally? Supposing Mrs. McKenna called the coach today and said, "Joyce, I hear you're going to help Kip Harlow become an Olympian."

No! Noni thought. Oh, no . . . *No!*

An aide came walking down the hallway. "Why aren't you in class?" she demanded. "Scoot off, or you'll get in trouble."

I am in trouble, Noni thought. Lots of it!

If only she knew Mrs. Balkans well, the way Denise Baxly knew her. Noni thought about that as she returned to study and opened her social studies book. It made her feel even more sour about Denise. She glowered at the other side of the room, where Denise, Marcie, and Brenda were sitting close together, giggling. Were they laughing about what had happened in science?

Never mind about science. Never mind about Denise and her creepy pals. What was she going to do about Kip?

I'll have to give it up, Noni thought. Mrs. Balkans would never . . .

A scrape of a chair pushed backward, footsteps.

A note slid in front of her. She read: "Did you get your brother into the Special Olympics yet?"

Noni whipped around. Denise was standing behind her. She wanted to shout, Get off my back! Instead, she found herself whispering. "How did you know about the . . . the Special Olympics?"

Denise dropped into a chair next to Noni. "I know Red gave you some booklets about the Special Olympics yesterday. Neill said you had them. He saw one, thought it was some brand-new athletic program or something. For normal kids."

Noni glared at Denise, hating her. Now Denise would blab. She and her pals would think up barbed things to say—sly little digs about swiftness running in the family.

"It's none of your business," she said. "What do you care what I do?"

"I know that there's a meet at Haymarket every year, around this time," Denise said, as if Noni hadn't spoken. "My mom was asked to give the awards last year."

That figured. The Baxlys of the world always won out and got awards, or gave them out. While Kip— To her horror, she realized that tears were filling her eyes, tears that Denise would despise as weakness. "Kip isn't going to enter any meet," she forced herself to say calmly. "There isn't any time, and there's no one who will train him." Now, she thought, go away! Go laugh about him! She turned her back on Denise, but Denise didn't budge.

"Have you tried Red Balkans?" Denise asked. Noni shook her head. "Why not? Too chicken?"

That did it! Noni snapped her head around, facing Denise. "Why don't you leave me alone?"

she snarled. "Is it hurting you to leave me alone? You want to laugh about something? Go right ahead. I wanted Kip to win something just once, okay? So he could . . . could feel good about himself. You're so damned selfish you couldn't understand that, but it's true. You didn't see Kip's face when—" she couldn't finish: when that little girl spat on him.

Noni wanted to put her head down on the desk and cry, but she wasn't about to give Baxly the satisfaction of seeing that. She was grateful when the study aide said, "Here, you girls over there! Knock it off and get back to work."

Denise left without another word, and Noni heard her whispering to Marcie and Brenda. She heard Marcie giggle, "How is the Running Nose?" and was astonished when Denise snapped, "That's old, Marcie, it's not funny."

Baxly sticking up for her? Noni was surprised. She also felt sick, after her outburst. She had so wanted Kip to have a chance, but it wasn't going to work. Let it go, Noni told herself. I tried. Let it go.

But that didn't help. She sat through the rest of her classes like a bump on a log. She thought she would feel better when school let out. Instead, she felt worse. School letting out meant going back home, facing Kip. It didn't help, either, when Denise came over to her while she was gathering up her books.

"Why not bring your brother to the school field around four?" Denise asked her. Why don't you take a flying leap to the moon? Noni wanted to reply, but Denise was still talking. "Red Balkans is going to be here around that time. She's asked me to stay. She wants to clock my speed."

"So?"

Denise put her hands on her slim waist and looked at Noni disgustedly. "So she can see your brother, look him over! Do you want me to draw you pictures, stupid?"

About to snap a reply, Noni stopped. "You mean you think . . . that Mrs. Balkans would agree to coach Kip?"

Denise shrugged. "How should I know? All I know is that she'll be here, and that you can talk to her, alone. You could show her what Kip can do. But if you think that's a waste of time . . ." Denise began to walk away, then paused. "I thought you wanted your brother to win something, just once. You're willing to cry about it, but not willing to do something about it, is that it?"

Noni found she was actually grinding her teeth. How she loathed Baxly! Yet, she was right. It wasn't much of a chance, but if Mrs. Balkans thought there was hope for Kip . . .

She owed Kip that chance, all right. If only someone else had suggested this—not Denise Baxly!

5

MOM HAD A HEADACHE. She was glad to be rid of Kip for an hour, to let him go off with Noni. "He's been restless all afternoon," she said irritably. "The RESCAB meeting took a long while."

"How did it go?" Noni asked, knowing it hadn't gone well.

"I'm sorry I went . . . it's not for me. Most of the women belong just so they can see their names on the committee." Mom's lips tightened. "A couple of the younger women brought their children along."

"Were they mean to Kip?" Noni asked, but Mom shook her head.

"They'd been coached to be 'nice' to the 'poor little boy,'" she said. She sounded awfully bitter, and Noni thought, Mom's angry, so nothing anybody does will work.

"I'll take Kip to my school, okay?" she said, then crossed her fingers behind her back as Mom hesitated. Say yes, Mom.

"It's pretty far," Mom said, and Noni held her crossed fingers tight, tight. "I suppose you could use the shuttle bus. That'll take you to within a few blocks of the school.

Kip loved buses. Noni was thankful that the town of Conan had the shuttle bus that came up and down Main Street once every hour. This bus was spanking clean and new, not scrawled over and battle-scarred like the ones in Lincoln. A lot of people turned around and stared when Kip started jumping up and down on the bus seat, but fortunately he soon tired of doing that. People stared out of the bus window.

"Tree," he sang to himself. "House . . ." His soft brown eyes glowed with excitement.

Unfortunately the enchantment didn't last. As soon as they got off the bus and started walking toward school, Kip complained that he was tired. "Go home, now," he announced.

Noni tried arguing, then coaxing, finally lost her temper. "This is all for you, you brat!" she exploded. Kip stuck out his lower lip, plopped down on the sidewalk.

"Want to go home," he insisted.

Noni sighed and began to reason. "Kippo, you like school. Don't you want to go and run races? You can meet my coach, Mrs. Balkans."

"No."

Noni sat down on the sidewalk next to Kip, hugging her knees. Time was passing . . . precious time! Had Mrs. Balkans gone home already? Or, maybe—this was an awful thought—maybe Denise had lied about Mrs. Balkans being at school in the first place. Maybe this was just a mean trick.

"Kip, please," Noni begged.

"No." His lips trrembled. Did he remember that awful incident at the track . . . the ribbon, those mean kids? "Go home," Kip pleaded.

Just then someone said, "Hey, Noni!"

It was Neill Oliver. He had his track stuff rolled into a towel, and his blond hair was rumpled.

"Just coming off practice," he told Noni, as if she didn't know boys had track Mondays, Wednesdays, and Fridays, and girls had track Tuesdays and Fridays, some Mondays. "I saw your coach clocking Denise." Neill's eyes brightened when he spoke of Denise.

So Denise hadn't lied. Mrs. Balkans was still there. Noni looked despairingly at Kip. "I was trying to get my brother to school, but he won't budge."

She expected Neill to nod and go on. Instead, he squatted down beside Kip. Sensing Neill's friendliness with his uncanny perception, Kip grinned.

"Hiya," Kip said.

"Hi, yourself. How come you're sitting down? Tired, huh?"

"Tired," Kip agreed.

"How about if I give you a ride?" Neill offered. "On the Oliver-mobile!" He made a vroom-vroom sound. Kip's eyes sparkled.

"Yea-ah! Vroom-vroom!"

"You don't have to—" Noni began, but Neill was already bending so that Kip could climb onto his broad shoulders.

"Watch it!" Noni warned. "He weighs!"

"So does my kid brother." Neill winced as Kip grabbed a hunk of his hair. "Hold on, Killer! Here we go . . . to school!"

"School!" Kip shrieked, in heaven. Noni felt happiness bubble through her as Neill started jogging down the sidewalk with Kip riding high. She jogged alongside them.

"A good way to train," Neill said, deadpan. Noni laughed. What would Denise say when the three of them came onto the school field like this?

Baxly did stare when she saw Neill and Kip. Then she turned back to Mrs. Balkans, ignoring them. Mrs. Balkans had a stopwatch in her hands, and she was talking seriously to Denise, pointing, nodding.

Noni turned to Neill. "Thanks," she said. "Really!"

"Anytime." Neill grinned, rubbed a hand in Kip's hair, and jogged off.

Noni looked after him, and so did Kip. "Vroom-vroom?" he asked hopefully.

"Not now, Kip. Look. Here we are at school." Ordinarily, Kip loved Noni's big school. Right now his lower lip stuck out again. "See that lady?" Noni said quickly. "That's my coach. I want you to show her how well you can run."

"Don't want to run! Vroom-vroom!"

"Kip!" Noni started impatiently, but he sat down on the ground rebelliously. Noni tried to lift him to his feet, but he went limp on her and hung in her arms, a deadweight. "Quit that!" Noni ordered, wanting to shake him. "It's not funny. Quit it!" Kip began to chuckle. "Listen, wise guy—"

But Kip was no longer laughing. His brown eyes were wide open, but inward-looking, as if he were listening to the sounds and movements inside his own body. He flopped down on the grass and lay there, staring up into the sky. Noni heard footsteps coming closer. No, she prayed . . . not Mrs. Balkans . . . not with Kip like this! But it was Denise.

"Red wants to talk to you," she said coolly. "I told her you'd be here with your brother." Then she looked down at Kip. "Ugh, gross! Is he having a fit or something?"

"He doesn't have fits!" But Noni couldn't be

mad at Denise's brutal frankness. Mrs. Balkans
was sure to refuse to take Kip on, seeing him like
this. He looked like a—a limp rag! "He'll come out
of it. Just leave him be!" Noni told Denise, who
was staring down at Kip as if he were some interesting bug.

"Noni!" Mrs. Balkans called. With a last, hopeless look at Kip, Noni ran over to her. The red-
haired coach was smiling pleasantly. "Denise told
me about the plan you two cooked up," she began.

The two of them! If it hadn't been so awful,
Noni would have laughed. My ally, Denise Baxly,
she thought.

"Denise told me about your wanting to enter
your brother in the Haymarket meet, Noni. She
feels I should look at what he can do," Mrs.
Balkans continued.

"Thank you," Noni mumbled.

"Now don't thank me till we see whether he
can do anything. You have to be especially care-
ful with—um—special children." She looked over to
where Kip was lying, and Noni's heart sank. "I
really feel I lack the necessary experience, but . . ."

Denise had come over to join them. "Go ahead,
Noni," she said to Noni. "Go get Kip."

Was Denise mocking her? Noni glared at her as
she went back over to where Kip was lying. He
wouldn't budge, wouldn't move—just wouldn't!
Noni begged and pleaded, ready to cry. It was no
use. He couldn't understand what any of this
might mean to him.

She went back to Denise and Mrs. Balkans.
"He's tired," she tried to explain. She saw polite
refusal building up in Mrs. Balkans' eyes. "If you
could just wait a little . . ."

Mrs. Balkans glanced at her wristwatch. "Well

. . . I do have a meeting I must go to. Just a minute, perhaps."

What good would a minute do? Kip lay so still. He was so motionless that a bunch of birds, sparrows, had landed beside him and were pecking in the grass for seeds and small bugs. They probably thought Kip was a stone, or a bundle of rags. Noni turned away, miserable.

That was when she heard Kip's joyous cry.

"Birds!" Kip yelled.

All of them—Noni, Denise, Mrs. Balkans—whipped around. They saw the birds take flight as Kip launched himself up from the grass. He lost his balance as he got to his feet, staggered, and then began to chase the birds.

"Bird, come back!" Kip called. His feet began to fly across the ground. "Birds . . ." He speeded up.

Noni's heart pounded like a drum. Run, Kip! she cried inside herself. The little boy ran on. When he stopped, still looking skyward after the lost sparrows, Noni realized she had clenched her hands into tight fists.

"He doesn't run badly," Denise, beside her, conceded. "What do you think, Mrs. Balkans?"

"He needs a lot of guidance," Mrs. Balkans said. Her voice was thoughtful, weighing some decision. Noni stared into her coach's face, suddenly hoping. Would she do it? Would she? Then Noni saw Red Balkans smile and knew the answer was yes.

"We don't have much time," Mrs. Balkans said. "We can't practice with Kip too long or too hard. It has to be a slow buildup of muscles. I take it he isn't used to exercising . . ."

Noni was so glad that she wanted to jump up

and down and turn cartwheels. She realized that Denise, too, was smiling, and that the cool, mocking look had gone from Baxly's face. The smile lasted for another few seconds. Then Denise seemed to catch herself.

"I expect speed runs in the family," she murmured so low that only Noni heard. "I'll bet you're glad I had the guts to speak up and tell Red when you didn't!"

Noni's hackles went up, but before she could say a word, her coach brought her down to earth.

"Has Kip had a checkup lately? I mean, a regular physical?" Mrs. Balkans asked.

Noni nodded. "Dr. Farrell examined him right after we moved to Conan."

"Well, that's fine, then," Mrs. Balkans said. "Now, I'll call your parents this evening. We'll—"

"Not my parents!" Noni blurted. They both stared at her. "They . . . they don't know yet."

"What do you mean?" Mrs. Balkans frowned. "You'd better explain, Noni."

Noni tried to. As usual, when things were important her tongue seemed to tie itself in knots. She wished that Denise would go away. It was hard trying to talk about secret, hurting things in front of her. "My mother's afraid Kip might get hurt—his feelings, I mean—if he loses," she stammered. "If you could train him, Mrs. Balkans, if you could show him how to win instead of lose . . ."

"Noni, I simply couldn't teach Kip anything without your parents' consent. You should know that! Not just because of Kip—though they probably know better than you or I about his capabilities and his emotions—but because of my position as coach at Conan Junior High." She looked regretful. "I'm sorry."

"Is there some way you could change your folks' minds?" Denise asked. Noni shook her head reluctantly. If she were more like Baxly, she could probably talk her parents into anything!

Denise seemed to read her mind, because she gave Noni a contemptuous look. You're giving up? the look said. I guessed as much . . . from you!

"If your parents change their minds, let me know," Mrs. Balkans was saying. "Kip could benefit from athletics—all kids can. Kip has potential, too. He's untrained, of course, but he runs well. He's fast." She patted Noni's shoulder gently, and began to walk away.

Denise hesitated, as if she were about to follow Mrs. Balkans. Then she stopped and gave Noni a look. "You're on the track team, aren't you?" she demanded.

"Of course I am! You know that. What's that got to do with anything?" Noni snapped.

"What has that do with anything? Only everything. Noni Harlow, you are sometimes so stupid you make me sick. You can train Kip yourself, can't you? You know how!" With that, Denise turned and loped after Mrs. Balkans.

Noni stared after her. Train Kip herself? The thought surprised, then scared, and finally excited her. Train Kip the way Mrs. Balkans had trained her team—could she do it? Yes, she thought, I can! I can work with Kip. And when Kip is trained, I can show the folks what he can do. They won't refuse to let Kip enter the meet then!

Or would they? For a second, Noni remembered the way Mom and Dad had looked last night when they had discussed the Special Olympics. She shivered. Then she pushed the thought away, looking over toward Kip, who was happily running around the track, pounding his heels down on the gravel and sending up little showers of dust.

She and Kip, they could do it together. They could. They *could!*

6

IT WAS EASY for Denise to tell Noni she should train Kip—easy for Noni to agree. She could even see how. There was an introductory booklet that had come with the literature Mrs. Balkans had given her about the Special Olympics. It showed the kind of exercises recommended for a workout. The question was—where?

Home was out. Mom was there. Noni had never worked out with Kip or even played with him the way she would have to, in order for Kip to get in shape within a few weeks' time. She wished that she had friends in Conan, someone she could talk to, but there was no one. Denise's brief helpfulness had disappeared into her usual snide behavior, and she totally ignored Noni at school. Noni was sure that Baxly was telling Marcie and Brenda about Kip, but though she waited all day for some cutting remark, none came. Apparently, so far, Denise hadn't blabbed.

Where? Noni continued to ask herself. Where? School was out, too. Kids hung around school for track, or baseball, or to wait for friends. They would see, and they'd ask questions, if she brought Kip to the school grounds to work out. Where else was there?

The answer came suddenly on Wednesday,

during science, while she was listening to Mr. Turello talk about pollution and oil-fouled beaches. That was it—the beach!

It was still too early in the spring for people to be out on the slender curve of Conan's beach. It wasn't that far from home. Kip could ride a bus to the beach with her, and back, and it would take only fifteen minutes each way. Kip loved the beach. That's it! Noni thought exultantly.

After school, she told Mom she wanted to take Kip to the beach. There was no fuss.

"How nice," Mom said, and Kip shouted, "Beach!"

"Don't tire Kip out," Mom warned. "Don't stay too long." She came to the door with them, looking out. "What a beautiful day. I almost feel like coming with you."

Noni's heart stopped beating. Don't come! You'll ruin it! she wanted to shout. Then, looking into her mother's face, she was sorry. Sunlight caught the gray in Mom's hair, the sadness in her eyes.

"Come," Noni said from a thick throat, but Mom shook her head.

"I need to do some work around the house," she said, and her voice, low and heavy, made Noni feel worse. Mom had been such fun in California. She and Noni and baby Kip had done so much together. Once they had gone to Corona Del Mar and pretended they were seahorses prancing in the surf. "Don't tire him, Noni," Mom said, sounding infinitely weary.

Noni felt depressed as they trudged to the bus stop and got on board. She wished there was a way to bring back the old happy times—the old mom, the old dad, and the sense of warmth they had had together before Kip was diagnosed. Perhaps, she thought, if he wins. If he starts feeling good about himself . . . Will things change?

She wanted things to change so much! Kip, she thought, you have to win and change things. Then Mom will stop looking bitter and Dad will be proud again.

Kip tugged her hand. "Beach? Birds?" he asked happily. He knew there would be birds at the beach, huge, white-winged sea gulls.

"Yes, birds. You can run races with the sea gulls, Kippy."

After a while, Kip said triumphantly, "Beach." They were there. Not that it was much of a beach—nothing like Corona Del Mar, or even Cape Cod right here in New England. But there was sand, and dunes, and sea . . . and privacy. Kip shouted with joy as a swoop of gulls rose into the air before him, and he stumbled through the sand chasing them. Noni followed, running too. It felt good to let the wind flow through her hair and around her. When she was running, she didn't feel awkward—all angles and bones. She felt . . . sure.

That would be the way for Kip, too!

"Okay, Kippo," she commanded, "stop running. I have a bunch of new games for you."

"Okay," Kip said agreeably, but his eyes followed the birds.

She taught him the "windmill," during which he turned his body in large circles, and the "airplane," where he had to circle his arms around and around. She did sit-ups and touching toes with him. Kip tried, and he did well, Noni thought. If only he wasn't so easily distracted! If a gull so much as appeared in the blue sky, Kip would forget what he was doing to jump up and point excitedly.

After about ten minutes of exercises, Kip said, "Birds now?" in such a longing voice that Noni relented.

"Sure. Okay. Go chase birds for a few minutes."

Kip jogged off, and Noni did her own warm-ups, wondering if she was going to be able to bring Kip out here tomorrow and the next day. It would be awkward, because on Friday she had track practice herself. If only there was somebody who could help. Well, she would have to manage about track and take care of Kip too, somehow . . .

"Noni! No-neeee!"

Kip's shriek slashed through her thoughts. Noni whirled, trying to locate Kip. He was nowhere in sight.

"Kip!" she yelled.

"No-neeee!"

What had happened to him? What? Kip's voice was coming from beyond a small dune. Noni ran as she had never run in her life. She was sure Kip was trapped . . . maybe in quicksand. Maybe he was drowning, or hurt! But when she leaped over the top of the dune, she saw him squatting in the sand in front of something dark and dirty, a handful of rags.

"Kip Harlow!" she yelled at him, relieved and angry and feeling shaky in the legs. "Why did you scare me out of my mind? If you ever do that again, I'll—"

"Noni, look!" Kip cried. He pointed to the yucky mess in front of him. "Bird!"

"Bird, nothing! It's a bunch of trash. You come with me right now and don't touch it. You'll get sick and Mom'll blame me."

She reached down to grab Kip's hand. The bundle of rags moved. Noni snatched back her hand and gave a gasp that was really a scream.

It *was* a bird.

Or it had been. Noni could see two angry, frightened red eyes peering at her through the mucked-up feathers. As she watched, a sharp, no-nonsense beak opened, snapped shut. The bird gave a strangled, snarling rasp of sound. It was warning them to stay away.

"Oil," Noni muttered out loud. Now she knew what was wrong with this bird. What had Mr. Turello said about birds being caught in the oil spill in the ocean? Birds with feathers gunked up by oil. Birds that tried to preen and died. She reached for Kip's hand again.

"Come on," she said, subdued. "The bird's sick. We can't do anything."

Kip pulled his hand away. "My bird!"

"For Pete's sake!" Noni exploded. "This isn't your bird! Don't start, that's all. Don't! Leave the bird and we'll do windmills, and we'll go home."

"Bird go home," Kip insisted. "My bird!"

Once Kip got hold of an idea, that was it. Noni glared at him. "I am going to walk over that sand dune and head back to the bus stop," she announced, speaking each word slowly. "You come after me, or you'll walk every step of the way home. Got that?"

Kip didn't say anything. He hadn't even heard her, or if he had, he didn't understand. Deliberately? Noni wondered bitterly as she turned and started stalking over the sand dune. He would follow her. Kip had a fear of being left in strange places alone. He would come in a minute, screaming. He would cling to her hand and whimper about the bird, but he would forget.

She reached the bus stop, but Kip did not appear. Why? She asked herself passionately. Why does this have to happen to me? Why didn't that dumb bird go die someplace where Kip couldn't find him?

A bus hove into sight and slowed to pick her up. Noni glanced desperately over her shoulder, but there was no Kip. Stamping her foot, she whirled and ran back over the dune, noticing how the bus driver was glaring after her. He thought she was playing a trick on him. She had caused a minor traffic tie-up behind the bus, too. Two cars, no less, had stopped so the bus could take her on board.

"Kip!" Noni bellowed. "Where are you? When I get you—"

She stopped. He was coming over the lip of the dune, planting his feet carefully. He was carrying something. Oh, no! He was carrying that gunky old bird! Carrying it in his arms. That bird could snap off his finger.

Noni wanted to yell, Drop it! but her voice wouldn't work.

"Bird come home," Kip said, nodding his head. He pressed his cheek to the filthy bird's head. It didn't budge and Noni felt a kind of awe. She wouldn't have had the guts to do that! She looked at the bird, which glared back at her fiercely. Why didn't the bird attack Kip or even struggle? It was uncanny.

A long time ago, she had read that wild creatures could sense fear in human beings, and that fear made them afraid, too. Could love be sensed? she wondered. Did this dirty, half-dead bird feel

Kip's love and acceptance and was that why it lay
so still?

"L'il Bird," Kip said.

Noni groaned. Kip figured this mess was a re-
placement for the lost canary!

"Kip, we can't take that . . . thing on the
bus. The bus driver would throw us off. What'll
Mom say when we get it home?"

Kip's eyes were rebellious. He was going to re-
tort, when Noni saw his attention shift to something behind her. Not something—someone. Neill
Oliver was running toward them.

"I thought it was you," he called. "We were following the bus when it stopped and you took off
down the dune. Mom and me were in Haymarket,
doing stuff, and she said she wanted to drive
home this way." He nodded toward Kip.
"What've you got, Killer?"

Kip held up the bird. Noni explained. "He
wants to keep it—ugh!"

Neill made no comment, but his eyebrows went
up. Finally he said, "You could take it to Mrs.
Baxly!"

"What?" Now Noni's eyebrows went up.

"No, really," Neill grinned understandingly.
"She's head of RESCAB, isn't she? She works with
all those birds and stuff. Denise is always talking
about the cleanups those nice ladies do." He
reached a cautious finger to the bird. It snapped,
beak closing millimeters away from Neill's hand.

"Oh," Neill said, impressed. "Wow! That's a
wicked beak he's got there."

"But it isn't biting Kip." Once more, the bird
settled against Kip's chest. "He won't let go of it,
that's for sure, and I can't ride a bus with it. Neill,

would your mother give us a ride to the . . . to the Baxlys?"

"I'll ask. I don't think she'll mind." Neill ran off, and Noni followed with Kip. Neill met them as they were climbing toward the road. "Mom says it's okay," he announced.

Mrs. Oliver was a big woman, large all over, even to her voice. "Watch it when you get in back," she warned Noni and Kip. "Move over, Eddie." Eddie was Neill's little brother, who cried out excitedly at the sight of the sea gull.

"Mine," Kip said, staking out his property.

"What a mess! Don't touch it, Eddie. It's likely to be a one-man bird. Right, Kip?"

Kip smiled sunnily. He liked Mrs. Oliver, just as he liked Neill. Noni liked her, too, even though Mrs. Oliver embarrassed her by saying, "So you're the gazelle."

"Pardon?" Noni asked, and Neill turned pink.

"Mo-om!" he muttered.

"Neill talked about the way you ran that 100-yard dash at the meet. Said he never saw such good form. High praise, Noni!"

Noni couldn't understand how she could feel so happy with things the way they were, but she did. Neill thought she looked good. That almost made up for having to face Mrs. Baxly with this awful-looking bird!

Neill offered to come with Noni and Kip to the Baxlys, and Noni accepted his offer gratefully even though she knew Neill was only making it so he could see Denise. Noni had a feeling Mrs. Baxly was going to have a fit when she saw the gull. They went around the back way and Noni knocked on the kitchen door.

Mrs. Baxly opened the door right away. She

gave Neill a welcoming smile while somehow managing to convey to Noni and Kip that they weren't so welcome. It was only when Noni began to explain about the gull that she noticed them at all.

"I don't know why you're bringing this . . . thing to me, Noni," she said.

"Well, you're the chairman of RESCAB," Noni said. She had a feeling that Mrs. Baxly thought that she, as well as the gull, was dirty and unwanted. Kip seemed to sense this, too. He clutched the bird tighter and stuck out his bottom lip. "We thought you'd know what to do, Mrs. Baxly. My brother found this bird on the beach . . ."

Mrs. Baxly peeked at the bird. "Ugh. I don't know what could be done for the poor thing. Maybe the Audubon people would know. There's a sanctuary on the Vineyard, you know. You could call the people there . . ."

"But . . ."

Noni looked at Neill, who said, "Maybe if you could tell us how to clean this thing up? I know there's a special method to clean oiled seabirds so they don't lose their water repellency. Mr. Turello told us what to use, but I forget."

"Fuller's clay." Noni hadn't noticed Denise standing behind Mrs. Baxly. "You have to use fuller's clay and rub most of the oil off that way. Then you have to use a really mild detergent. Right, Ma?"

Mrs. Baxly looked bored. "I doubt if it would do any good. Most of these birds. don't survive, even after being cleaned. This one seems weak." She looked at Kip. "Put it down, little boy."

Kip just gaped at her.

Mrs. Baxly frowned. "Does he understand?" she asked Noni.

"Yes, he understands—" But before she could go on, Kip gently lowered the bird to the ground. Neill hunkered down beside it.

"Neill, it's going to die in a few hours, anyway," Mrs. Baxly said. "See? It can't even stand up."

"No, it's not dying . . . it's the legs. See, Mrs. Baxly? The legs look funny. They're broken, I think."

"Well, then!" Mrs. Baxly's voice rose triumphantly. "It would never survive, I assure you. It's much kinder to put a creature like this to sleep. Even if such a bird should return to its kind, they would kill it. Only the strong survive."

Noni saw Neill look at Denise. As if *she* had an answer, Noni thought resentfully.

"It's a gull," Neill said. "If it were cleaned up, the wings would be white."

Suddenly Denise spoke up. "We have some fuller's clay left over from that RESCAB cleanup, Ma. What do you think, Neill?"

Neill grinned. "I think it's worth a shot."

"For heaven's sake!" Mrs. Baxly snapped, but Denise looked at the bird, then at Noni.

"Help me find the clay, Noni," she commanded. "Neill will stay here with Kip and the bird."

Noni followed Denise in surprised silence. How many months had she lived on this street, and this was the first time she had been invited into Denise's house! Why was Denise acting so friendly? Probably because Neill was around and Baxly wanted to appear great.

And great was the word for the Baxly home. Elegant. It was completely color-coordinated, even to Mr. Baxly's study. The study, Noni saw as they passed, was lined with books, certificates, diplomas. Denise's room was like that too.

Noni was awed. She had known Denise was good at sports and at school, but she hadn't known how good! Denise's walls were covered with ribbons and medals, photos of Denise on winning teams, certificates of achievement from school. On a gleaming bedside table stood two silver cups, sports awards. No wonder Denise was a leader, the captain of the track team, and of everything else.

"Here it is," Denise announced. "It was in my closet." She held out a brown paper bag to Noni, who took it without a word. "It'd take too long to explain just how to clean that bird. I'll help you."

Noni could only stare, speechless. *I'll help you.* The last words she had ever expected to hear from Baxly.

7

NEILL SAID he would help, too. "But where can we do it?" he asked. "Your garage, Noni?"

Noni wasn't too sure of Mom's reaction. "I'll ask," she said.

But it was Kip's asking that turned the trick, not Noni's explanations. And he didn't say a word, just stood there, cradling the bird against his chest, looking at Mom with his big brown eyes. Mom, who at first cried out against Kip touching—never mind holding—"that thing," who refused to let it anywhere near the house or the garage, changed her mind when she saw the bird and the boy together.

"Would you believe it? And that's a wild creature," she murmured, to herself. "It's as if it knows . . ."

Knows what? Noni asked herself grumpily. The only thing she knew was that it was going to take some doing to clean off the bird.

"Can I use the garage, Mom, is it okay?" she asked.

Mom nodded yes, and Noni went to get old towels and Kip's baby bathtub, filled with warm, gently soaped water. All that time Mom kept watching Kip and the bird. She kept shaking her head.

And well she might. It was a job getting the oil off the bird's feathers. The fuller's clay had to be rubbed through the feathers, then brushed away together with as much oil as would cling to the stuff. The bird didn't help. It was too weak to fight much, but what it could do, it did. Even though they all wore thick work gloves, scrounged from Dad's work area in the garage, the bird left its mark on every one of them.

Or, everyone except Kip. "My bird," Kip insisted, beaming.

The look on her brother's face kept Noni from throwing in the towel and wringing the fool bird's neck! Not only was it incredibly fouled by the oil, but the legs *were* broken—no doubt about it. Noni hated to admit it, but Mrs. Baxly could be right. It was useless cleaning up a crippled bird, a bird that would never survive, anyway, unless . . .

"If only there was some way to splint its legs," she finally said, when the bird was as clean as they could get it and lying in a towel in Kip's arms. "How long would a bird's legs take to heal?"

"I don't know. Maybe a couple of weeks." Denise pushed back her long blond hair and puffed her cheeks. "It's not going to stay still for you for two weeks, Noni."

"I know that." But the way Denise had worked, getting nipped and clawed, the way she had patiently scrubbed oil and gently lathered the bird made it impossible for Noni to resent the scornful words. She sighed. "Maybe your mother was right."

"Ma is almost always right." Denise's voice had an edge to it. "I was hoping that she wasn't right this time, that the legs weren't broken, but

. . ." She shrugged. "There isn't much choice, is there? We have to . . ." She let the sentence hang.

Neill wiped his hands on his jeans. "Maybe we could figure a way of putting this character in traction," he said. They looked at him. "I'm serious. I once read about a bird—a falcon, or something. It broke its legs, and this lady actually splinted it with paper tubing and tape. Let me think!" He pressed his fingers to his temples, concentrating. "I think this is the way she did it. First, she made a hammock—"

"A hammock!"

Neill frowned at Noni. "Yeah . . . a hammock! It was a canvas hammock, I remember, and she slung it between two stakes. The bird sat on the hammock with its legs hanging down out of two holes she made in the canvas. Then she splinted the legs."

"But didn't the bird try to pull free?" Denise asked, interested. "A gull has strong wings. It could hurt itself trying to get free. Or tear the splints off its legs."

"Not if we hammered another stake into the ground underneath the hammock and taped the gull's legs to it," Neill explained.

They all looked at each other silently. In the stillness Kip crooned to the bird, a song without words.

Noni broke the silence by saying, "I have some denim upstairs. I got it for sewing, but we could use it for a hammock. It's strong."

"Would your mom let us use the garage? The floor isn't concrete or metal, so we could pound stakes into the ground." Neill was excited.

"Gulls eat anything, not like some other birds.

There'd be no problem feeding it." Denise's face was flushed. "Let's do it, Noni!" she cried.

"I'll go ask. Mom has to say yes!" Noni almost flew as she ran to the kitchen and Mom. When Mom said she had no objection, providing Noni cleaned up after the bird, she leaped up the stairs to her room, taking two, three steps at a time. By the time she returned to the garage, Neill had found a hammer and a saw and was making stakes out of wood scraps. Kip sat, wide-eyed, enthralled by what was happening He rocked the gull in his arms.

Neill pounded the stakes into the ground. "That'll hold a skyscraper," he boasted. "Just call me the John Henry of Conan."

The girls groaned, and Noni found herself grinning at Denise—a real, genuine, friendly grin. Denise smiled back.

"Boys always get the easy jobs," she said. "Girls do the jobs that need brains."

She was right, in a way. The hammock was harder to devise. Noni and Denise turned the sturdy denim cloth several different ways before deciding to cut it on the bias, folded twice over to give added strength. Then they hooked one end around one stake, secured it, and tied another loop around the second stake. They left it up to Neill to punch holes in the hammock where the gull's legs would go.

Then came the roughest part of all—splinting the gull's broken legs. They used Noni's old Girl Scout first-aid book as a manual, paper-towel tubing, and plenty of tape. The tubes were too fat and had to be scaled down, and reams of tape were wasted. Fortunately, the gull had hardly the strength left to struggle now,

At one point Noni despaired. "Maybe we should call a vet. We're getting this all wrong."

"There's no vet in Conan. Besides, he would just say what Ma did—to put the gull out of its misery," Denise said firmly.

Maybe the gull's legs would never mend, Noni worried. Maybe they would have to kill it later, because they had set the legs all wrong!

But when the job was finished, the bird looked better than she had hoped. It sat on its denim hammock, legs splinted and taped to the block of wood wedged securely between its feet. It squawked and protested, but quieted when Kip brought it food—cubes of bread soaked in water, and some sardines. The bird ate eagerly, snapping up the food.

"The way to this turkey's heart is through the stomach. Who said that?" Neill laughed happily.

Noni giggled, feeling good. "Now, I'll have to explain to Kip—really explain—that this bird can't be turned loose before it heals. I guess he'll have to sit like this for at least two weeks."

Neill nodded, gave her back an approving pat.

"You've got it, Noni," he said, his voice warm with approval. Noni felt as if she had turned her face toward the warm spring sun. "I'd say that Kip has the magic touch with this bird. You guys shouldn't have any trouble. Anyway, I'll be around to look old Bird up."

"Great!" Noni cried, but Denise got up, gracefully.

"Come on, Neill," she said smoothly, "let's go clean up over at my place." Noni started to offer her own bathroom, but Denise then added, "See you, Noni!"

Neill hesitated and looked at Noni as if he realized how Denise had suddenly cut her out of the partnership. Then he said, "Later," a little awkwardly and followed Denise. Noni watched them go. She felt a core of aloneness deep within her, especially as she watched Neill reach out to lace his fingers through Denise's. Why had Denise done that? she wondered, knowing the answer.

Denise couldn't stand anyone else's having the limelight. She had resented, just now, Neill's offer to come and see the bird. If Neill came to see the bird, he would come because it was Denise's idea.

Boys are so dumb! They couldn't see a thing inches past their own noses. Neill thought Denise was the greatest. He couldn't see the selfish streak, as wide as the Mississippi, running through her.

Noni realized that Kip was standing beside her. "He's her boyfriend and you're my problem," she sighed. "How can I be so lucky?"

8

So MANY PROBLEMS, Noni thought as she headed for track practice—so many aggravations! They had led her to make a decision she had never believed she could make.

Almost a week had passed, and the coming of the bird had added, not taken away, problems. Problem number one was Mrs. Baxly. Well, not a problem—an aggravation. After all the work and thinking had been done, Mrs. Baxly had stepped in and taken the credit for cleaning the gull and saving it. She had actually had the gall to tell the RESCAB committee that *she* had suggested a way for the sea gull to be healed.

Mrs. Baxly had also stuck her nose in to tell Noni she needed a special license in order to keep the gull. Then she used her "influence" to get the license, maintaining loudly that this was for a "special little boy." If that wasn't sickening enough, the Conan *Herald* got into the act and wrote a feature about Mrs. Baxly entitled "A Lady with a Heart." There was a big photo of Mrs. Baxly printed with the article, and that made Noni want to barf.

Mrs. Baxly aside, there was another aggravation—Kip. It was nauseating how his world began and ended with Bird, as he called the gull. He was always in the garage, patting, touching, talking to the creature. And feeding it! The gull wouldn't take food from anyone but Kip, but it wasn't suffering. Noni figured that if things continued on their present course, the bird would end up the fattest gull alive. And who cleaned up the mess of droppings Bird deposited on the garage floor each day? Well, guess who!

There were other messes, too, like this Special Olympics thing.

Sometimes, like today, Noni wondered how she ever got mixed up in everything. She had her own practice to go through, and then she faced an hour of frustration with Kip. Kip simply wasn't interested in training. Not only did he refuse to leave Bird for an instant, he soon tired of doing excercises and drills. It was hard working out in the garage, anyway, and the garage was the only place where Kip would consent to do anything at all.

It might have been different if Kip had other kids to work with. It would have been different if he had had another coach. She wished she dared to tell Kip about the meet and his big race, the race that would win him a big gold medal, but Noni knew Kip wouldn't be able to keep a secret. He would blab to Mom.

Noni chewed her lip. She was fresh out of ideas and needed help, and here was where the big decision fitted in. Today at track practice she was going to ask Denise for help. She had thought about it, and it seemed the only thing to do. Denise knew a lot more about track than Noni did, and Noni also kept remembering how gently Denise had washed Bird's oil-fouled wings. Maybe Baxly wasn't so bad after all!

Denise had mellowed since the day Neill, she, and Noni had worked to clean Bird up. Though Denise made a point of being right there whenever Neill came over to see how Bird was doing, she hadn't done anything mean or snotty to Noni for a long time. More, she had kept her snickery pals, particularly Marcie, off Noni's back. Often Noni would catch Denise watching her, her eyes questioning. How are you coming along with Kip? those eyes seemed to ask.

Noni drew a deep breath. Well, here it was, the moment of truth! She glanced over where Denise stood with Marcie and Brenda, wishing Denise were alone so she could talk to her before Mrs. Balkans arrived for practice. But Noni was too late. Mrs. Balkans had come onto the field, and she was waving something in her hand—a brown manila envelope.

"Noni!" she called. "This came for you from Haymarket. Jean McKenna sent it, care of my office at the school."

It had to be the forms Mrs. McKenna had promised to send! Noni hurried over, wishing nosy Marcie and Brenda weren't listening in. She hoped Mrs. Balkans wouldn't say any more, but the coach asked, "I hope this means you've talked your parents into changing their minds about your cute little brother?"

"Cute!" Brenda said, making a face. Marcie stuck her tongue out, knuckled her knees, and made her eyes roll.

And Denise laughed. She *laughed* at Marcie—at Kip!

Stabbing black hatred for Denise boiled up in Noni, more fierce than anything she had ever felt before. And she had been on the brink of asking

Denise Baxly for help! She had been about to trust her!

How could she laugh! Noni raged. How could she laugh at Marcie when she had seen the way Kip held the bird? How *could* she?

Fury made Noni run faster that day. Mrs. Balkans was delighted. "Keep it up and you'll break all the school records, Noni, including the ones Denise set last year!" she encouraged.

Noni glared at Denise and got a cool so-what look back. She would break Baxly's records, all right. Yes, she would! She would break them as if they were Baxly's bones. She was that mad.

She went home angry, the forms Mrs. McKenna had sent still unread in their brown manila envelope. She didn't feel like reading the forms now. Hatred for Baxly burned into everything she did, made her snarl at Kip and talk back to Mom. Mom said she was getting too big for her britches.

"What's wrong with you, looking like a thundercloud with your mouth hanging down to there? You shape up, Noni Harlow. Now!"

Noni flung herself out of the house, mad, hating Denise, hearing Denise laugh. Denise was the one to shape up, not Noni!

A while later, Mom shouted that she had to go to the grocery store. "You mind Kip, do you hear? And try to look a little more pleasant!" Noni just glared at the ground and returned to her hating as Mom left the house.

"Noni?" She felt a little nudge behind her. She didn't turn around. "No-nee?" Kip pleaded. She turned, looked into his wide brown eyes, and saw he had brought her a peace offering. He was holding the envelope Mrs. McKenna had sent. "For Noni?"

She sighed. What was the use? She couldn't be mad at Kip. And anyway, it wasn't his fault. "Thanks, Kipps," she said.

Relieved that she didn't have any mad feelings anymore, the boy trotted over to the garage and Bird. Noni held the envelope loosely in her hands a moment, then slit it open. Forms tumbled out—a medical form, a parents' release form, an entry form, and a letter.

The letter was from Mrs. McKenna to Noni. Noni skimmed the bold handwriting. "Any help I can give . . . wonderful program, have been involved in it for years . . . I myself have a brain-damaged son, Georgie, about your brother's age . . . send the forms in as quickly as possible, since we don't have much time."

Noni read these last words a second time. "Kip!" she shouted.

Kip stuck his head around the garage door. "What?"

"We have to practice. Yes, we do! You come out of that garage!" She wasn't going to go into that stinking garage, not when Mom was gone and they could work out here! Kip reluctantly emerged. "Do the windmill!" she ordered.

Kip's face told her he didn't want to do any windmill. He didn't want to touch his toes, either. Noni kept after him, while mulling over what she should do next. With no one to help her, there was no place she could go. She would either have to tell her folks or quit. Without her parents' signature on the parents' release form, without Dr. Farrell's name on the bottom of the medical form, Kip couldn't enter the Haymarket meet.

"Keep those feet kicking!" she shouted. "Don't you *want* to be a winner?"

"You sure work him hard," a man's voice said behind her.

Noni turned sharply. It was an older man, about Dad's age, with a dusting of gray at the temples. He had a camera around his neck, a briefcase tucked under his arm, and he stood on the sidewalk beside a dusty green Ford.

"I'm Jacob Hansen—Jake—from the *Sun*," he explained. "Can I talk to you and your brother a minute?"

The *Sun*? The Lincoln city paper? Noni blinked at him and then at the press card he handed her. She glanced over at Kip, who was watching with interest.

"What about?" she asked carefully.

"About the bird and your brother," Jake Hansen explained.

Noni frowned. Mom wouldn't want her to talk to a stranger. The man shouldn't even be here while she and Kip were alone. But they weren't really alone, Noni reasoned. Neighbors were around. She could see people in their backyards, working on spring gardens.

Kip came over to Jake. He held out a hand.

"Hi," he said acceptingly.

Noni felt herself relax. She had faith in Kip's uncanny ability to sniff out the good or the bad in people. She felt even better when Jake hunkered down on his heels and took Kip's hand, smiling not with his mouth, but with his eyes. He has kind eyes, Noni thought.

"I don't know," she said, however. "I don't think my folks want Kip interviewed or anything." She added bitterly, "Why not talk to Mrs. Baxly? She likes to see her name in the paper."

"She the one who encouraged you kids to save

the bird?" Noni looked sour, and Jake grinned. "I read the article in your local paper. Wasn't that way, huh?"

"No. She told us to go wring Bird's neck."

"Suppose you tell me about it," Jake said. Kip ran to the garage to where Bird sat, and after a second, Noni shrugged and led Jake Hansen into the garage, too.

"There he is. Bird. Ta-daa!"

Jake began to ask questions. Before long, Noni realized she was chatting away easily, telling Jake about how she and Kip had gone to the beach, how he had scared her to death by screaming for her. "His attention wandered, see. He got tired with his workout—"

"Workout?" Jake asked.

And because he had asked so quietly, Noni found herself answering. "Sure. For the Haymarket meet—" Then she stopped. "That's not important, anyway," she added hastily. "I thought you wanted to talk about Bird."

Jake asked more questions about the bird, writing it all down in a notebook. Then he took photos—of Kip with the gull, and then of Noni, Kip, and the gull.

"I smelled a human interest story somewhere," he said with satisfaction. "I didn't think it'd be this good."

Just then, Mom called Noni's name. She was standing outside the garage, bundles in her arms and a frown between her brows. Jake Hansen's press card didn't take the frown away, but his easy manner relaxed her as it had relaxed Noni. He even got a smile out of Mom when he assured her that a photo of Noni, Kip, and Bird would be in the *Sun* soon.

"I bet Mrs. Baxly will have a fit," Noni giggled as Jake drove away. That actually made Mom laugh out loud.

"I'm sure she will. She'll probably claim that the whole story is a fake." She headed for the house, humming under her breath, and Noni helped carry in groceries, thankful that Mom was in such a good mood.

If she remained in a good mood till tonight, if Dad had a good day at work, there was a chance her parents might listen to her. Noni's thoughts slid back into the pattern that had been interrupted by Hansen's coming. Tonight she would tell her folks about how she had worked with Kip. She would try to make them see how much Kip could do, that Kip could be a winner.

Let Dad be in a good mood, Noni prayed. Please!

He wasn't. Dad returned home late, with taut explanations about having had a "talk" with his boss. He had been called on the carpet, blamed for something another employee had done. "And you didn't speak up?" Mom demanded. Her voice rose shrilly. "Don't you have any self-respect left, Jim Harlow?"

Dad said nothing. The meal was eaten in stillness, cold and chill and brittle. Noni despaired. She just couldn't force herself to call attention to Kip in this angry quiet. Yet she had to. There was no time. Mrs. McKenna's letter had told her how little time was left. Noni felt as as if the walls and the ceiling and the floor had turned into an accordion and were squeezing her close. I have to, she thought desperately.

"Hey," she began, her voice unnaturally loud. "I was thinking—"

"Don't start a conversation with 'hey,'" Mom said sharply, and Noni subsided. She glanced over toward Kip, who was chasing his meatloaf around on his plate with his fork.

"Quit that!" Dad suddenly rapped out. "Can't you eat properly?"

Kip's face crumpled, and Mom's head went up as she said coldly, "He eats as well as he can."

"Really? How would you know? How would you know what he can or can't do? You won't let him try!"

They were going to start. Noni felt like shouting, Don't! She wanted to beg them to stop, but she knew it was useless. The storm was coming.

"So it's my fault, now? My fault that he was terrorized at that awful place in Lincoln? You and Mary insisted he go—"

Dad smacked his hand down on the table. "At least I don't try to coddle him and hide him from the world!" he roared.

Into the silence Noni heard herself blurt, "Do you know that Kip can run real fast?"

They stopped hassling, both of them, and looked at her. Their eyes were blank, angry from the fight that was just beginning, but at least they were looking at her.

"Yes, he's really fast!" Noni gabbled. "Mrs. Balkans said so. I've been thinking. If he entered that Haymarket meet—"

Crash! Mom dropped her fork onto her plate. Kip started to cry. "Are you still beating that dead horse?" Dad demanded bitterly. "Your mother won't even try to send your brother to the Haymarket school. Do you think she'd let him run a race there?"

Noni couldn't look at Mom, but surely her face was as grim as her voice. "Don't you have any homework, Noni? Take Kip up to bed when you go. He's overtired," Mom said.

Noni didn't wait around to be told a second time. Shaking, she got up from the table, went over to the still-crying Kip and took his hand. She tried to say, Come on, Kippo, but her voice had gone someplace, along with all the words she had wanted to use to convince her folks. As she and Kip started up the stairs together, she heard her mother speaking, her voice, low, tense, angry. Soon, her parents would blame each other about Kip—prod, hurt, taunt.

It's getting worse, Noni thought, her heart thumping painfully as she pulled Kip up the stairs. It'll get worse and worse, and then—

And then, what?

She didn't want to think of it, but she did. Several kids in California had had divorced parents. So had kids in Lincoln. She was sure that many kids in Conan Junior High had parents who had split up.

And then . . . divorce?

It was bad enough as it was now, but divorce? Noni couldn't take it in. She took Kip to his room, helped him undress and get on his jammies, and put him to bed. His round, scared eyes told her that he sensed her fear, and she tried to smile reassuringly, even though her mouth kept jumping in an ugly way.

Noni shut off the light in Kip's room and went to her own room. She tried to close her door against the sound of angry voices downstairs, but she couldn't. Dad was shouting and so was Mom, and neither of them was listening to the other.

They didn't want to listen. They were riding their own private hurts, moving farther and farther apart. If only, Noni thought desperately, there was a way to get them back on the same track again.

Like making Kip a winner. That would unite them again, wouldn't it? Wouldn't it unite the whole family if Kip won?

Tears gritted her eyelids, and she felt terribly alone and scared. Then, as she started to move toward her bed, she heard Dad yell, "All right! It's my fault for putting him into that program in Lincoln! But let me tell you something, Dina. I thought I was helping Kip. I'd do anything to help him along, to give him some pride in himself. I'd go and . . . and commit a crime if I had to!"

Noni's eyes fell on the forms Mrs. McKenna had sent. They were lying on her desk where she had put them.

"Pride in yourself, you mean!" Mom wailed. "You want to make Kip into something he can't be!"

Stop it, stop it! Noni ran over to the forms, grabbed them, and nearly threw them into the trash. Then she stopped.

Commit a crime, Dad had said. He hadn't meant it, of course. He was just talking from his anger. No crime he could think of would ever help Kip. But Noni could think of one. She looked down at the forms in her hands, at the empty form with "signature" printed underneath.

Forgery!

"No," she whispered out loud, "I couldn't. It wouldn't work, anyway." But the thoughts formed in her mind, building up force. Supposing I filled out the release form and the medical form. Supposing I filled out the application form? I could do it. I could copy the stuff off the paper Dr. Farrell gave us when Kip had his last physical. That paper has Dr. Farrell's signature, too.

But . . . copy the doctor's signature? Forge her parents' names? Noni's hands felt damp and sweaty as fragments of earlier thoughts darted in and out of her brain. Unify the family. Do anything to have pride in Kip. Then she thought, I must hurry . . . hurry! Mom keeps Kip's records and stuff in her bureau drawer. I have to get those papers quick, before they come upstairs.

She opened the door to her room, stood there listening. Mom was crying softly. "You can't accept him as he is," she whimpered. Noni couldn't hear her father's reply. She could only hear the sound of her heartbeat thundering in her ears as she hurried across the dark hall into her parents' room. Her fingers, clammy and clumsy with panic, fumbled as she pulled open her mother's bureau drawer, took out the file on which Mom had printed: "Kip's Medical Records."

Noni turned on the night-light in order to see better, and slid the top paper away from the others. Yes, there was the stuff she needed to copy, and Dr. Farrell's signature.

"You tell me to have pride. How can I?" It was Dad's voice, and, oh, glory, it was coming nearer! He was coming up the stairs! Noni felt sick as she quickly pushed the file back into the drawer, shut off the night-light, and scuttled into the hall. Her heart was pounding so hard as she got back to her own room that her whole rib cage moved. She had never felt this scared—or this guilty!

Dad's footsteps came up the stairs, crossed the

hall. He had stopped in front of her door! Was he coming in? Had he heard her in the other bedroom?

The door opened.

"Noni." Noni couldn't move but she felt a great relief. Dad didn't sound mad. He sounded . . . sad. "I'm sorry you had to hear all of that," Dad said.

Noni shook her head, unable to speak. Dad went on, "Nobody is angry with you. You do understand?" Her numb neck nodded. "It's just . . . your mother and I disagree about what's right for Kip. She wants to protect him. Maybe I push him too far." His shoulders hunched even lower, and Noni wanted to run to him, hug him. "I can understand why you want him to compete in this Special Olumpics thing, but it's out. Try to see why."

He closed the door to her room gently. For a long moment, Noni just looked at the closed door. She wanted to cry, and yet she knew it wasn't going to help a thing if she cried.

As if she had wakened out of a deep sleep, she turned to her desk and put down the paper she had taken from Kip's medical file. Pulling a piece of paper out of her school notebook, she began to practice writing Dr. Farrell's signature.

9

ALL NIGHT the forged forms tormented Noni. She had put them in her desk after filling in the blanks and signing, first her father's, then Dr. Farrell's name. They lay in an envelope addressed to Mrs. Jean McKenna in Haymarket, and she was going to mail them in the morning.

There was a mailbox by the school bus stop. She left earlier than usual in the morning, walking at first very fast, then, as she drew nearer the mailbox, very slowly. I have to do it, she told herself, but still she hesitated. The mailbox slot was a huge mouth, grinning at her, as she lifted the envelope up to it.

She heard footsteps coming down the sidewalk, and saw Denise walking toward the bus stop. Noni gave the letter a push, and it fell into the mailbox with a sickening thump.

Noni felt a lot sicker at school. She felt terrible. Her stomach ached and so did her head, and during English she threw up. The school nurse sent her home, thinking she had a bug, but Noni knew better. They were doing a scene from Shakespeare's *Julius Caesar* in English class, and a line from that play stuck in her mind now, "Thy evil conscience, Brutus!"

My conscience isn't evil, Noni insisted to her-

self. I'm doing this for Kip, and for the family!
Then why did she feel slimy, vile, when Mom
tucked her into bed so concernedly? When Mom
called Dr. Farrell, all worried, and brought her
ice cream to eat, she felt worse. Do you know
what I just did? she felt like yelling.

She stayed in bed all day. It was the easiest
thing to do, so as not to have to look at or talk to
anyone. Later in the afternoon, she felt guilty
about not putting Kip through his workout, until
Kip had company—Neill Oliver. Neill came over
with some tuna for Bird, and she could hear Neill
and Kip laughing over Bird's greediness.

With Neill around, Kip wouldn't miss his workout. He won't miss me, either, Noni thought, and
tears of self-pity oozed into her eyes. She could
hear Kip's high voice calling, "Vroom-vrooom,"
and knew Neill was giving Kip an Oliver-mobile
ride again. Sure, Kip liked Neill. Neill never
yelled at him, or kept after him to do exercises
and run in a straight line. But Neill wasn't the
one sick at his stomach because he had committed
a crime for Kip! Weakly, Noni wondered when
Mrs. McKenna would get the forms. Not for a day
or so, anyway.

Mom didn't let Noni go to school the next
morning, either. "You had nightmares all night
long. I could hear you tossing and mumbling,"
she said, when Noni dragged herself out of bed.
"If it's the 24-hour bug, let's give it time to die a
natural death."

Noni didn't mind staying in bed at first, but she
felt much better today. After a while, she got so
bored she dressed and went outside, where she
stayed most of the morning and early afternoon,

watching Kip do his thing with Bird and feeling the warm spring sun on her back.

Sitting like this, thinking of very little, Noni lost track of time. She was surprised when she saw Neill loping down the street. Was it that late? She thought he would stop at the Baxlys', but he continued on past Denise's house and jogged down into the Harlows' backyard.

"Hi!" Neill flopped down beside Noni. "I thought you were sick."

"I was." She wrapped her arms around her knees, pleased that he was there. Then she saw Denise come out of her house and stand on the porch, and her brief pleasure disappeared. "Aren't you supposed to be over at Denise's?" she asked. "She's watching us."

"So?" Neill frowned.

"She might get mad." Noni had to keep her anger at Denise bottled up so she wouldn't say too much.

Neill didn't say anything. He lay down full length on the grass beside Noni, closed his eyes, and propped his arms behind his head. He looked thoughtful. "You know," he said, "she's an only child."

"Denise, you mean?"

"That's the reason she's the way she is. She's a cool kid, but she always has to be number one in everything. She got so mad that day you won the 100-yard dash. I sort of understood at the time, but . . ."

Noni heard the critical note in Neill's voice and knew she should be ashamed because it made her feel so happy. He's finding out that Miss Baxly isn't Miss Perfect America, she thought. "I thought you guys were going together," she said carefully.

Neill made a grunting noise that could have meant yes or no. "Don't get me wrong, I think she's great. I just wish, sometimes, she'd relax, and just—"

"Nora!"

Mom's voice exploded the peaceful afternoon like rifle fire. Noni whirled, saw Mom standing on the back steps, a folded something in her hand. The look on Mom's face made Noni's blood go all icy. Mom never called her "Nora," either, unless—

"Nora! Come here this instant!" Mom shouted.

Neill looked at her with startled eyes. Noni stumbled to her feet and forced a smile. "She's mad at me for something," she said to Neill. "Be right back." She then walked toward the back door, heart pumping wildly. Now she could see what Mom was holding in her hand—this evening edition of the *Sun!*

"I want you to look at something," Mom said, deadly quiet. She held the kitchen door open for her daughter, swung it closed behind them both. Noni saw that she was white around the lips. Mom had never looked like this before. No, she had too! That day Kip had run away in Lincoln and had been found cowering in that alleyway!

"Read!" Mom commanded, thrusting the newspaper into Noni's hands. The letters danced in front of Noni's eyes and she could hardly make them out. Then she saw the photograph of Kip, the bird, and herself. Underneath the photo were words: "Little Kip Harlow . . . Noni's brother . . . Noni training her brother for his first big race at the Haymarket meet for special children . . ."

Oh, no! she thought. No . . .

She remembered that it had slipped out about training Kip, when she was talking with Jake Hansen, the *Sun* reporter. He had picked it right up, of course. He had wanted a human interest story. She skimmed the lines, feeling worse as she read how Jake had compared Kip to the wounded bird—paralleled Bird's struggle to get well with Kip's determination to win his race at Haymarket.

"I am going to call the *Sun*," Mom was saying grimly. "I am going to tell them what I think of their comparing my Kip to a crippled bird. Hasn't Kip been hurt enough without people seeing him as some hopeless cripple?" Her finger stabbed. "You did this to him, Noni!"

Noni shook her head. "Mom, no, you don't understand . . ."

"Don't tell me, no! You did this to him! I told you to forget about that Haymarket thing, but you went right on with it, didn't you? Behind my back! You were training Kip for a race behind my back! And I thought you were being so kind, so loving, playing with him every afternoon." Mom pushed her face closer to Noni's. "Was that what you were doing with Kip all these afternoons after school? Training him like a . . . a performing seal?"

Noni felt her body letting go, sliding into a pool of mush. Her mind felt like a jigsaw puzzle someone had scrambled up. Helplessly she shook her head. It wasn't like that.

"Get out of my sight!" Mom ordered. "I'm too mad to talk rationally right now."

Noni left the kitchen, a burning in her chest. I want to cry, Noni thought incoherently. I want to disappear. She headed blindly outside, then realized that Neill was sitting in the grass with Kip.

She couldn't face either of them right now! She went up to her room instead.

There was nothing to help her there. Her room offered no refuge from Mom's face, the tone of her voice. *You did this to him,* she had said. And, *comparing my Kip to a crippled bird . . .*

Noni barked her shins on the bed as she went to lie down. She felt heavy with tears that just wouldn't flow. Things had been bad enough, now she had made them worse.

There were sounds underneath her window—car sounds. Screeching brakes and then a slamming car door. A second later Noni heard Dad's voice.

"Where is she?" Dad was demanding.

Where is who? Noni wondered. Me? As if in answer, she heard Dad's raised voice calling, "Noni! Come down here!"

She would not go down. She couldn't take any more. She'd be sick again . . . yes, sick, right here and now! Noni swallowed the sour taste of her own fear and misery and heard murmured voices downstairs.

"Nora! Did you hear me? This instant!" Dad roared.

I won't. I can't . . . But somehow she was up and walking to the door. Turning the doorknob with hands that felt numb, she walked out onto the landing. They were standing at the foot of the stairs, waiting for her—Dad, Mom, and . . . Mrs. Balkans! What's she doing here? Noni asked herself before she realized that the forms she had sent Mrs. McKenna must have reached Haymarket.

The forged forms!

"Noni . . . how could you?" Dad was asking. She had expected rage and condemnation, but not the pain in Dad's voice. She couldn't find her voice. "Come down here," Dad said.

Stiffly she went down the stairs. "We're waiting for an explanation," Dad said, and then he himself began to explain. "Mrs. Balkans called me at the office to congratulate me for entering Kip in the Haymarket meet. She wanted to set up some mutually agreeable training schedules for Kip. It seems that someone sent parental release and medical forms to the director of the Haymarket meet—"

Mrs. Balkans broke in. "Dr. Farrell never signed that medical release form, did he, Noni?" Slowly—she seemed to be doing everything so slowly—Noni shook her head and Mrs. Balkans got all red in the face. "You amaze me, do you know that? You really do. You have total disregard for anyone but yourself! What about my position at the school? Do you realize that you were jeopardizing my job? And what about the people who've been working so hard to make the meet at Haymarket a success? Didn't you stop to think that you could ruin it all for them?" Noni blinked at her. "Yes," Mrs. Balkans stormed. "Ruined! Supposing Kip got hurt? Don't you think that could have made it hard for them to hold meets like this again?"

"And you never thought of what it could do to Kip," Mom snapped.

"I did it *for* Kip." Noni had wanted to shout it, but it came out in a whimper. "I wanted him to win at the meet. He could have . . ."

Sadly Dad said, "No, Noni. He couldn't have done anything like that. You have to understand how limited Kip is."

Now the shout came, filling her lungs with anger. "*You* don't understand!" she cried. They looked shocked dumb for a moment, and she raged on. "Kip could win. He's good! How do you know he isn't good? Have you worked with him? Have you even tried?"

"Noni—" Mom began, but Noni had gone too far to stop now.

"He's never won anything, don't you see? He's never been on top, not once! I wanted him to be able to . . . to *make* it, just once!"

"But to forge signatures!" Mrs. Balkans' voice was uncertain. "I can certainly understand why you did this. But you realize that you acted very wrongly. Forgery is—"

"Stop talking about *me!*" Noni stormed. "It's Kip we're talking about!" She stumbled past them, banging into walls and doors in her blind hurry to get outside. "Kip!" she called. "Kip!"

They had to *see* the progress Kip had made. She had a confused glimpse of Neill standing next to Kip and staring at her, and of Kip's face, stunned and scared. She forced herself to calm down and talk in a normal voice. "Kippo, I want you to show Mom and Dad how well you can do the windmill."

Kip didn't move. Don't let him be stubborn, Noni pleaded silently, and somehow Kip must have understood how important this was. He began to go into his workout, the one they had done every single day together. He did windmills, and the airplane, and then touching toes. Noni was shaking all over. Her teeth chattered as she directed Kip. At any moment she expected her folks to stop the workout, but nobody breathed a word.

Then Noni said, "Kip, run!"

Kip ran. He ran the way Noni had shown him,

the way Mrs. Balkans had shown Noni. He ran pretty straight, and he was fast. Kip smiled, showing how good he felt about running. Noni felt tears grit her eyelids as she heard Kip's clear, sunny laughter. Kip, she thought, it's not true what they say. You're no loser—you never were!

"Stop!" Dad said in a low voice. "That's enough. Stop."

Kip stopped running and collapsed on the grass next to Neill. He shoved at Neill's legs, playfully, giggling. Neill didn't move. He was staring at Noni with his mouth practically hanging open. "You taught him all that?" Neill demanded. "By yourself?"

Noni nodded. Why didn't her folks say something? "There wasn't anyone else who could teach him," she mumbled.

"Oh, wow!" Neill sounded impressed. "Hey, Noni, maybe you should help coach *us!*"

Then Dad broke the silence. "You did all that in just a few days, hiding in the garage."

Mrs. Balkans shook her head. "The boy has potential. Athletics certainly would help him. I saw that at once, but when Noni said you were against the idea of his competing . . ." Her voice trailed away.

Noni held her breath, not looking at Mom. Mom was the one everything hinged on. For a long while, Mom said nothing, watching Kip, who had gotten tired of all these staring adults and was heading back to the garage and Bird. Then she said, "That was why you were sick yesterday." There were tears in her eyes. "Poor Noni. Poor baby . . ."

Mom put her arms around Noni and hugged her. Noni felt the tears, held so long inside her, break loose. But still she wouldn't let herself cry. "He's good, Mom—isn't he good?" she insisted. Only when her mother nodded, slowly, did she let the sobs come. Her whole body shook with them.

"Reaction," Mrs. Balkans said, and made Noni sit down with her head between her knees. Stupid to cry now, Noni thought. Why cry when it's all over? But she gasped and sobbed until Mom brought her some ammonia from the kitchen and made her smell it. Mom was wiping her own eyes.

"It's all right," she said. "It's all right."

And it really was, because Dad asked, "Is there still time, Mrs. Balkans, to fill out proper papers and forms for Kip? To train him in the correct way?"

Noni held her breath until she heard her coach say, "It's late, but then Kip has had good training already. I certainly could help him . . ."

"So could I!" Neill piped up. "We all could help."

"Yes, by God!" Dad's voice made Noni come around much faster than the whiff of ammonia. "We can help Kip win." The pride . . . the newborn pride in Dad's voice told her everything was going to be all right.

10

" 'Happy days are here again!' " Going to
school Monday morning Noni could have sung,
shouted, yelled the words. Instead, she just
hummed them softly, hugging her happiness.
" '... Are here, are here, are here again.' "

They had sung that song yesterday, all the way
to Haymarket and all the way back. Dad and Kip
and Noni had sung, and Mom had drummed her
fingers on the dashboard in accompaniment, a
soft, relaxed smile on her mouth.

" 'Happy days are here again!' "

This was how it felt to get to heaven while you
were still alive. Everything was working out the
way she had prayed it would—even better. Golden
days seemed to spill into nights of cozy content,
evenings of no hassling, no angry locked-in
feelings, no tearing tensions. Dad and Mom didn't
yell at each other anymore. They talked. They listened.

Mom had listened when Dad really wanted to
drive to Haymarket yesterday to see the school
and meet Mrs. Jean McKenna. She had been a
little hesitant, as if unable to let go all of her fear
for Kip right at once, but she had gone.

Kip loved the school. They had been allowed to
walk through empty classrooms, together with

Mrs. McKenna, who had arranged this visit for them. They had seen the places where children learned arts and crafts, or concentrated on self-expression, or pridefully did chores.

"It's a nice school," Noni remembered Mom saying slowly and Mrs. McKenna touching her arm.

"I know how you feel, I truly do, Dina. But it has been wonderful for Georgie." Mrs. McKenna had smiled at Mom. "We're going to work very hard to get Kip into school as soon as humanly possible, all right?" Mom had only hesitated a moment before nodding, and Noni couldn't help shouting.

"All *right!*"

Kip liked Mrs. McKenna, too. Who wouldn't? She was slim and pretty and friendly without being gushy, and she had three kids—Helen, who was Noni's age; Georgie, a year older than Kip; and baby Ed. Georgie was brain-damaged, but he certainly held his own. He was dead set on winning the softball throw at the Haymarket meet, and Noni was sure he would. After the visit to the school, the Harlows had gone over to Mrs. McKenna's for lunch, and Noni's hand still smarted from the fastball Georgie had thrown her.

Georgie would make it, and so would Kip. Noni was sure of it. Not just sure of Kip. We all will make it, she thought.

Like Mom. Aunt Mary had called Mom a couple of days ago, just after everything had come out in the open. "You're a great fool, Dina," Aunt Mary had scolded. "Kip will never be able to take the pressure of the crowds. He'll run away as he did here in Lincoln. I'll bet he can't even understand what 'race' means."

Mom held her own. "He most certainly does understand. We've explained it, and he saw the high school track in Haymarket where he's going to compete. He was thrilled. Besides, Mary, there will be no pressure. Special Olympics is geared to make kids think better of themselves, not just compete!" Bossy Aunt Mary had dried up!

Then Dad got into the act as well. Last night at supper he had talked about convincing his boss to help at the Haymarket meet. "He's had some experience playing basketball in college, and I told him he could probably help out with the basketball clinic they're having the day of the meet," Dad said. "I told him it was for my son and for other kids like Kip." There was pride in his voice, for himself as well as Kip. "Of course he agreed. He's heard what Noni has done."

Noni could have hugged herself, wanted to hug herself, now. I did this, she thought. I pulled it off. It still shocked her, whenever she thought how quickly things had moved after her secret came out.

Neill had something to do with it. He had gone to Mr. Crusoe, his coach and Mr. Crusoe had called up Jean McKenna to volunteer his time as a referee and to help with the track clinic. Then the Conan Junior High boys' track team had volunteered to help out at the Haymarket meet—building stands, coaching, whatever.

It hadn't stopped there. Mrs. Balkans had told Kip's story to the other teachers at the junior high, and the news spread like wildfire. Before she knew it, kids who had never spoken to Noni were coming up to her, telling her what a great thing she was doing, and offering their help. Even

Brenda and Marcie, Denise's pet pals, had congratulated Noni. She still felt stunned by that.

And it had snowballed further, from the junior high to the whole town. Within days, everyone knew about Kip. High school students, parents, neighbors, and strangers on the street were speaking to the Harlows—encouraging, wishing them luck. It was like opening the front door expecting winter and finding the first day of spring.

Still that wasn't all. Kip's story did something else for Conan. Three other kids, retarded like Kip, were going to compete in the Haymarket games for the first time. Their parents had been reluctant to enter them as Olympians before, but, as one lady told Noni, Kip's story had changed their minds.

"We've lived here in Conan for years and years," she said. "I've known about the Haymarket games, but I never thought to enter my daughter in them. Then I heard how hard you worked to get your brother entered in the games, and I decided to try."

As it stood now, Mrs. Balkans, Mr. Crusoe, and selected members of both boys' and girls' track teams worked with Kip and the three other kids every day at the junior high gym. Neill worked with the boys, while Noni, Brenda, and another girl worked out with the girls. Mrs. Balkans had asked Denise too, but she had refused.

Denise. Noni didn't want to think about Denise—not now, when every other thought was pure happiness. She couldn't help it, though. She could see, in her mind, Denise's shuttered and cold face. Denise had come to her the day after the article about Kip had been printed in the *Sun*, and Noni could still hear Denise say, "You think you're so great, don't you? Everyone's talking about you. I suppose you think you did this all by yourself?"

But I did! Noni meant to cry, yet something in Denise's eye made her stop. Denise *had* helped. Before Noni could say so, though, Denise added, "I suppose Neill and I didn't help you with that filthy bird? *You* took all the credit. I suppose *you* talked Red Balkans into seeing your brother? Oh, you're so clever, Noni. I'm sick and tired of hearing how clever you are!"

Then she had walked away, leaving Noni staring after her, uncomfortable and angry because Denise was trying to ruin things for her again.

This time, however, Denise ruined things for herself. That same afternoon, Mrs. Balkans had asked Denise to help with training the girl Olympians and Denise had shaken her head.

"I'm sure you'll have plenty of help without me. Noni's such an experienced coach!" Then she added, "I have other things to do."

Mrs. Balkans was shocked. "Denise!" But Denise had already stalked off. "Well!" Red Balkans exclaimed. "I never expected that! The idea of being so rude."

"I'll help, Mrs. Balkans," Brenda spoke up. "I never figured Denise to be such a poor sport. I thought she was a pretty neat kid, till now."

"Denise just likes to boss people around. She's mad because Noni thought of this idea, not her!" Marcie added, and Noni, looking at her, wanted to cry, But you're her friend!

"I'm really surprised." The way Mrs. Balkans said that, Noni knew Denise would never get back the coach's respect. When Marcie and Brenda spread the story around the school, a lot of other people who had considered Denise to be smart and pretty and really all right in every way were also surprised. Then there was Neill. Noni had heard that Denise and Neill had had a fight over this Haymarket meet.

Noni began to hum again, dismissing the thought of Denise. Why bother about her? If Denise had problems, she had brought them on herself. Noni squared her shoulders, threw back her hair, and drew in a deep, wonderful breath of spring air. Life was pretty good and going to get better. Once Kip won his gold medal a few days from now, the happy days would be here to stay!

11

"Hey, Noni!"

"What d'you say, Noni?"

"How's Kip today?"

She couldn't put names to all the friendly faces that turned her way as she walked through the school building to her first class, but the greetings made her smile, gave a bounce to her step, made the song she had been singing bubble through her till she couldn't keep from grinning all over her face.

Someone fell in step with her—Brenda. "Kip's really coming on well, isn't he? Those other kids, too. With us coaching, how could he not win?" Beside Brenda, Marcie gave a thumbs-up sign.

Noni nodded, feeling uncomfortable. She always felt strange when Brenda and Marcie acted buddy-buddy, especially Marcie. She remembered all the cutting things Marcie had said when she was Denise's pal. Lately, Marcie didn't even look Denise's way, and she said cutting things about Denise.

Now, for instance, she said, "I heard something you might want to know, Noni. Guess who had a big fight over the weekend?"

Noni shrugged. Marcie grinned and leaned

closer. "Denise and Neill," she announced. "Neill finally realized what a gross person Denise is."

"You can't blame him," Brenda drawled. "She's just a snob. Look at all those trophies and ribbons she collects in her room. I bet she just went out with Neill because he's a Big Man in Track, and because it was a cool thing to do. I bet Denise never even liked him. She can't like anyone but herself."

"Just like her mother," Marcie said cuttingly. "My mom says that all Mrs. Baxly wants out of life is to see her name chairing every committee in this town. Like mother, like daughter."

They were both looking at her, and Noni felt even more uncomfortable. Marcie and Brenda were looking at her the way they used to look at Denise, looking *up* to me, Noni thought. It was a funny feeling. She enjoyed and disliked it at the same time.

"Denise isn't all that bad," she heard herself say with a dumb little laugh.

"Look at the crummy things she said about you," Brenda pointed out. "That dumb things about the Running Nose. She said stuff about Kip, too, don't you remember?"

So did you, Noni thought. "We'll be late for class," she said. She wished that Marcie and Brenda would walk with someone else and quit talking about Denise and the old, sad days. She didn't want to think about them.

But Marcie wasn't going to shut up so easily. "If you ask me," she said slyly, "I think Denise is jealous. Neill likes someone."

She looked at Noni in a way that made Noni ask, "Who?"

"Who do you think?" Marcie puffed her lips,

narrowed her eyes. "Who's he been spending all his time with, huh?"

Brenda winked. "Don't you know Neill likes you?"

Her cheeks blazing, Noni protested, "It's for Kip."

"He likes *you*—that's why he's helping so much with your brother! Don't you know when a boy likes you?"

Marcie's voice was bantering, but slightly envious. Noni felt her breath catch in her throat. Neill liked her? But no one had liked her before—no one like Neill, anyway!

They walked through the classroom door, Marcie still chattering on about Neill in her ear. Noni looked around the classroom, seeing that Neill hadn't yet arrived. Someone else was there, however, sitting alone, chin propped in her hands, looking down into a book.

Denise.

She looked . . . well, lonely. The thought shocked Noni. The sight of Denise Baxly, who had always, always been surrounded by friends and admirers, sitting there and pretending to study, the way Noni herself had often done, bothered her. Noni bit her lip and watched Brenda walk past Denise, ignoring her completely.

Marcie went a step further. "Someone's brains are working real hard. I smell rubber burning," she said in that snickery voice Noni remembered so well. Denise didn't even move. "I guess she's deaf as well as dumb," Marcie said in a loud whisper.

Noni sat down two seats away from Brenda and Marcie. She watched the determined straightness of Denise's back ahead of her. When

Neill came in, Denise's ramrod-stern posture didn't crumple. Neill smiled at Noni, but ignored Denise. Then it was true, Noni thought.They did have a fight.

A fight over me? Because Neill likes me?

She thought about that as science started. Hadn't Neill come over just because of Kip? True, he had come more and more often lately, and they saw each other after school a lot because they were both working with the Haymarket meet kids in the gym. Noni remembered how Neill always came over to talk to her during breaks in the training program. They had talked about school, track—nothing personal. Yet it had felt good to be so close to Neill, to stand looking up into his clear blue eyes, listening to the voice that had just now begun to change.

Would other things change? Noni wondered. Suddenly her excitement wavered, turned to unease. If Neill liked her, if she liked him back, would the good feelings between them change? She had heard so much about being in love, but what did that mean? She suddenly felt angular and awkward, all legs and bones. She wasn't built slender and pretty like Denise. Then how could Neill . . .

"Noni." Mr. Turello sighed. "He was shaking his head at her, and she realized she had missed hearing another one of his questions. She braced herself for Mr. Turello's sarcasm, but today he just smiled. "I suppose I have to forgive you for daydreaming, Noni," he said in a really quite kind voice. "Working with those kids must take a lot out of you, eh? Your brother's entered for the 50-yard dash, isn't that so?"

"Yes, Mr. Turello," Noni managed, and the science teacher's smile broadened.

"My money's on Kip to win. We're all with you, Noni."

The class turned around and smiled at Noni. We're all with you, Noni.

Denise didn't turn around.

Forget Denise, Noni told herself. Who needs her?

Noni didn't need her, that was for sure, not now! Whether she liked it or not, Marcie and Brenda stuck close to her. During lunch, Neill came to sit with her, and other kids crowded around Noni's table. During class, things were that way too. In home room, when they discussed an upcoming eighth-grade party, Noni's name came up first to head the committee. Even in study, aides came up to tell Noni they had heard about what she was doing and to wish her well.

Neill teased her about it. "You're a celebrity," he told her during last period. "Going to give me your autograph?"

"Sure. How many would you like?" Noni kidded right back. The teasing words seemed to come easily now. There was no more mind-groping, no numb shyness! Neill grinned.

"At least a hundred. I'll sell them after the Haymarket meet and get rich."

"Hush!" The English teacher was glaring at them.

"See you after school?" Neil whispered. "I have track practice, but just for a second before you get on the bus? I want to talk to you."

Noni nodded and saw that there was a pale flush of pink on Neill's cheeks. The excitement-uneasiness that had begun in her this morning came back. He wanted to talk to her. He wanted to talk to her about . . . what? Her cheeks felt hot.

Noni couldn't wait for the buzzer to sound. Neill gathered up his books and sauntered into the hall to wait for her. Noni hurried so she could follow him. She was moving toward the door when she felt herself jostled aside.

"Look where you're going, clod!" Denise snapped.

"You're the one who should look!" Noni shot back. "I didn't even see you!"

"You never could see much, anyway," Denise said. Her voice was angrier than Noni had ever heard it. "You're sightless and brainless."

Noni bristled. "Just what is it with you, anyway?"

"You think you're so-o special. All these dumb creeps running after you because they think you're something else. Well, you make me sick."

Noni tried to step past Denise to where Neill was waiting for her. She didn't have to stay here and listen to this! Denise saw Neill and her face flamed.

"I'm going to tell you something, Noni Harlow. You took all the credit for this business with Kip and the Special Olympics. That's okay with me. There are glory hounds on this earth. What makes me sick is that you're twisting it." She stopped, pulled in a ragged breath and went on, "When you started out, you wanted to do something for your brother, you really did. It was something unselfish. I actually admired you for that."

"Denise, are you crazy? Of course I'm doing this for Kip."

"Are you? Stories about you in the paper.

Teachers talking about you in the teachers' lounge—yes, I overheard them! 'What one girl can do, it's amazing!' " Denise mimicked. "I'm sick up to here hearing about you. Even Ma started talking about you at home. And you love it, don't you? You eat it up. Pretty soon you're going to believe you're as great as everyone says you are. You think you're God's gift to Conan."

Noni felt blood whooshing, roaring to her head. "Talk about glory hounds!" she snapped. "What about you? What about your trophies and ribbons and . . . and your mother? Look how she took credit after we'd saved the gull—"

"Don't you say anything about Ma!" Denise looked as if she were going to hit Noni.

"Get out of my way or I'll push you out of it!" Noni ordered.

They glared at each other for a long moment. "All right, your Majesty, Queen Noni the Jerk!" Denise stammered, she was so angry. "Sure, I'll get out of your way, you creepy hypocrite!"

Noni wanted to take handfuls of Denise's bright, fair hair, and twist and pull. Instead, she walked away from Denise, toward Neill. He was waiting for her, eyebrows raised.

"What was all that about?" he asked. Noni realized he hadn't heard what they were saying to each other.

"Denise is mad at me. She thinks I'm a hypocrite." Noni clipped her words angry-short. "She says I make her sick."

"I guess she's mad at the world." A shrug dismissed Denise. Neill fell into step beside Noni, as they walked down the corridor. "I wanted to tell you I won't be up at the gym to work out with the kids today."

It was so different from what she had half expected to hear that Noni just stared. "You . . .
won't?" she asked.

"I can't come today." Again, Neill's cheeks were
pink.

Noni felt a strange tightening begin inside her
chest. Was Marcie wrong? Perhaps Neill liked
someone else! She looked up at the tall boy and
thought, I wish they hadn't said anything to me
about his liking me. Now, if he likes someone better than he likes me, I won't be able to stand it!

"See," Neill explained, "I have to mow the
lawn. Mom said she'd pay me a few bucks to do
the front and back, and there's this lady down the
street who wants her place mowed too." He
paused and added shortly, "I need money.
There's a good movie downtown . . ."

He started telling her the story of the movie.
Noni nodded, not hearing one word in ten. Why
was he telling her about a dumb old movie?
Unless he wanted her to go with him?

". . . thinking that after Kip wins his gold
medal this Saturday, we could sort of celebrate
and go see the movie," Neill was saying. He
glanced at her. "We could catch the seven-to-nine
show."

He was asking her out! Noni floundered briefly,
then mercifully Neill added, "My folks wouldn't
let me go to the later show on a . . . a date."

"That's my parents, too." Thank goodness for
parents! You could talk about them when you
were too embarrassed to think of anything else to
say! "So dumb!"

"Probably they think we turn into vampire bats
after ten." Neill made a vampire face.

They both laughed, and the prickly, excite-

ment-uneasiness disappeared. Noni felt herself
again, and she wanted to reach out and take
Neill's big hand in hers. She was too shy to do it,
but she had a feeling that when she did, it would
feel natural, that the broad, strong hand would fit
comfortably and gently around her own.

Liking someone was pretty nice. It wasn't scary
at all.

Neill reached out and touched her cheek
lightly. His eyes were reflecting her own thoughts
back to her. "You're really kind of special, Noni,"
he said softly. "Really."

12

NONI RODE the bus home in a dream, reliving it all. Neill's touch on her cheek. His smile. The words that made her feel special. Then she let go of those dreams and lived forward, till Saturday, and Neill.

It wasn't till she got off the school bus that she came down to earth with a bang. It was Denise's stop too, but the blond girl waited till the last possible moment, till the bus was almost moving, so as not even to have to look at Noni. When she did get off, she swooped past Noni, head up, nose in the air, as if Noni was completely beneath her notice.

It should have made Noni laugh, but it didn't. It bothered her.

She couldn't understand why. She hadn't said anything cutting or cruel to Denise. And it was so unfair—Denise's implying that she, Noni, was a glory hound. The publicity that surrounded Kip wasn't of her making. All she wanted to do was to help Kip be the winner he could be. It was unfair ... and sick. Baxly was sick.

Forget it, Noni told herself, but she couldn't. Watching Denise swish along the sidewalk ahead of her, walking alone as Noni herself had walked so often, she couldn't forget it. She remembered an old story about a cat who walked by itself. That was Denise—an angry, lonely, spitting cat. And cats had claws.

Claws? A dumb thing to think of. Baxly couldn't possibly do anything to her. Anything she had done, like refusing to help train the kids, only backfired, making her look bad. So why worry?

"Noni?" Mom's call cut through Noni's thoughts. Mom was standing in the front doorway, waving. "Noni! Hurry, dear! Grab a snack. We're supposed to be at the gym in fifteen minutes!"

Grateful to stop thinking about Denise, Noni jogged the rest of the way home. Mom gave her a hug as she came up the front steps, and the smile on her face had California sunshine in it.

"You look happy," Noni said to Mom.

"And you look as if you have something on your mind," Mom came right back. Noni knew she had to watch herself. Mom was with-it again these days, and she could pick up mood changes in the family. It was almost like the days before Kip was diagnosed! "Is it Denise?"

"Well, kind of." Noni went over to the kitchen table, found it piled high with brownies and a chocolate cake.

"The brownies are from Mrs. Oliver, and the cake is from a neighbor. They want Kip to keep up his strength for his race."

"Kip will get too fat to run—like Bird." Noni cut herself a piece of cake.

"That's not what Mrs. Balkans says. She says Kip will run rings around everyone." Pride lay heavy in Mom's voice. "But now that you mention it, I want to talk to you, Noni, about Bird."

Noni took another slice of cake. "What about him, Mom?"

"Mrs. Baxly came by today," Mom said. "She told me that it's time we released Bird, because his legs would have healed by now. A crime to keep wild creatures penned up—that was the way she put it."

"Oh-h," Noni groaned. "Don't do it, Mom, not till after the race, anyway. Don't listen to her."

"Of course I won't. I told Mrs. Baxly that we'd keep Bird with us a little longer, to be sure he was well, and also to keep Kip happy till after the big meet. Then we can set Bird free in celebration." Mom's eyes were on the garage. "The way Kip talks to that bird—as if he thinks it's human! I didn't realize how lonely he's been, Noni. Once he starts school though, he'll have other kids to play with. He won't need Bird anymore."

Mom stopped talking, but she said something else, softly, under her breath.

"What did you say?" Noni asked.

"Just that all of us need something to love and to believe in." Tears suddenly starred Mom's eyes. "Noni, it's hard to tell a pretty grown-up daughter but—Dad and I love you. I guess you know how much pride we have in you, too."

Noni ducked her head. "C'mon," she muttered, embarrassed, but pleased too.

Mom laughed. "Well, you sure woke up the town of Conan! And made Aunt Mary dry up too. When I told her about you, she didn't have a word to say." She rested a hand on Noni's shoulder. "Whatever Kip will do this Saturday, he owes to you. If you hadn't jolted us awake—"

She stopped talking as Kip came galloping into the kitchen. "Bird hungry, Ma," he said.

"There are sardines in the refrigerator. Then wash your hands, Kip." Kip nodded. Since the exercises, since Bird, since the good feelings had come back, Kip was responding so much better! Maybe he wouldn't be like other kids, Noni thought, but he'd be okay. No one would ever spit on him again, or could take this Saturday's medal away from him.

And it's because of me. Take that, Baxly, and hang it in your ear!

"Now, Noni, about what's bothering you." Noni shrugged. "Is it Neill?"

"How did you know?" Noni gasped.

Mom laughed. "Well, he's been hanging around here a lot these days. I wondered how long before he got up enough nerve to say something."

Noni told Mom about the movie, and Mom looked thoughtful. Noni had an awful thought— Mom would surely let her go? But then Mom said, "Well, I think fourteen is rather young for a date, but this is a special occasion. We'll drive you down and maybe Mrs. Oliver will pick you up." Then she added, "You're responsible kids, after all."

Saturday, Noni thought. She felt so full of excitement she was sure she was going to burst. She jumped up from the kitchen table and ran outside and did five sprints around the house, just to work off the bursting-out happiness. Saturday . . . the race . . . and Neill. It was all coming true at once!

As she went back into the house, Noni happened to glance over her shoulder at the Baxlys' house. Denise was standing on her porch, watching Noni, but she neither moved nor spoke. She looked neither mad nor sad. She looked as if she were waiting for something to happen.

13

Noni knew that when you are waiting for a day to come, the hours crawl by inch by inch, like snails.

Monday had been an up day. Friday was down, all the way. Everyone was nervous and tense, from Bird all the way up to Mrs. Balkans. Bird sat in his hammock and yarked at everyone, even Kip. Friday afternoon Mrs. Balkans lost her peppery temper and shouted at Kip for not listening and concentrating.

"Will you stop thinking about that stupid gull and listen to what I say?" Red Balkans demanded. "Tomorrow is the race! It's important! How will you win if you don't listen?"

Kip looked at her out of wondering dark eyes. "Kip win," he repeated softly.

Noni could see Mrs. Balkans melt. She groaned, patted Kip's shoulder. "Take ten, Kip, I need a rest," she said and went to stand against the gym wall. Noni went over to her. Behind her, Mr. Crusoe and Neill, together with another boy, were training the other little boy who was entering the meet, while Brenda and some other girls worked with the little girls. "Oh, that's fine, Rennie, fine!" Noni heard Brenda say encouragingly.

Mrs. Balkans puffed out her cheeks like a red-

103

headed chipmunk. "I'm not nervous about tomorrow, am I?" she asked, beginning to laugh. "It's too bad I yelled at poor Kip. But he can do it. I know he can. I want him to run his heels off. I want so much for him. I want him to go to the regionals, the state, the national ..."

"I know." Noni wanted the same things too. "Can Kip do it?"

"Yes, he can, if he concentrates. I get the feeling that all he wants to do today is to go home and play with that dratted bird. What you are going to tell him when it comes time to set the bird free I'll never know." Mrs. Balkans pushed herself away from the wall. "Well, back to work."

Noni felt tingly with nerves as she watched Kip go through his warm-ups again and jog around the gym. Pride in Kip's new confidence, his improved posture and speed, wrestled with nervous, whining thoughts inside her mind. Supposing, the whining thoughts whispered, he doesn't win? Supposing he gets disoriented, or scared by the crowds? What'll you do it those awful things happen, Noni?

Of course Kip would win! No question. Yet perhaps it was bad luck to keep thinking about the race. Noni heartily wished that tomorrow would come, come quick, and get over with so she could relax. So everyone could relax!

Mom and Dad were taut with race fever. They were irritable and sharp with each other, had been for a day or so. Noni knew it was because of the tension. Mom was torn between pride in Kip and a last-minute attack of nerves. "Are you *sure* it won't be too much for him?" she kept saying, till Dad, last night, had exploded.

"Dina, for Pete's sake, don't start coddling the

boy all over again!" Later he was sorry. "I just wish Saturday was over," he sighed.

Amen, Noni wanted to agree. She herself was sharp-tongued at school. She had snapped Marcie quiet earlier in the day when Marcie tried out one of her snotty jibes on someone. "Can't you ever say anything nice?" Noni demanded. Marcie, frowning, had retreated.

"Noni, you're getting to sound like Denise," Marcie had said.

Noni sensed the warning. Sharp-tongued Marcie was better kept as a friend than as an enemy, but right now Noni couldn't care less. After the race, when she could think again, she would stop acting so bad-tempered.

Didn't people realize it was because she was so concerned about Kip? Even Neill had been upset with her earlier that day.

"All you can think about is the race," he had flared. "All you can think about is Kip winning!"

He actually glared at her. "I told Denise she was crazy when she said you were obsessed with making Kip win, but now I don't know. You *know* that winning isn't the idea of the Special Olympics, Noni. The meet's held so that kids can do their best, not so they can get hung up on winning!"

Noni hadn't been able to believe her ears. "Is that why we've all been working on Kip? So he can lose?"

"No, and you know it!" Neill kicked the ground explosively. "Oh, forget it. I just wonder what would happen if Kip lost . . ."

Watching Neill's long, lean figure at the other end of the gym now, Noni chewed her lip. She hated to have this mad feeling between her and

Neill, but she felt tangled up, as if her nerves were a snarled skein of thread. How could Neill talk about Kip losing? Kip couldn't lose. He was good, he was fast, he was Conan's darling. The whole town was behind him.

"Kip!" Mrs. Balkans was coaxing. "Come on. Run for me!"

But Kip, sensing the nervous currents in the air, turned whiny, and couldn't, or wouldn't, do anything right. Finally, Mrs. Balkans gave up. "Just as well he relaxes today and gets a good night's sleep," she told Noni. "You know what they say—bad rehearsal, good play."

Noni knew she had to relax so that Kip could also. His divining-rod mind drew from her uneasiness, sensed her worry. But how to relax? Making up her argument with Neill helped.

"I know we're both uptight," Neill said to Noni as she and Kip waited for Mom to pick them up. "Look, my folks are going to the meet tomorrow, but I thought maybe I'd ride along with you guys. I could help keep Kip loose."

Noni thanked him. "We'll leave around nine thirty, I guess." She sighed. "I wish it was over. I wish I could relax!"

Neill grinned. "We'll relax at the movie tomorrow," he promised.

But even that didn't help right now. Uptight—that was the word for them all, though Noni thought that *down*tight was a better description. "Hush," she told Kip, when he started whining. "Just hush!"

Kip didn't hush. By the time Mom picked them up, he was querulous and uncooperative. He wouldn't eat his supper, balked at his bath, refused to go to sleep. Dad lost his temper, but Mom knew what was wrong.

"We're making him nervous," she said. "He senses it in us, and it bothers him."

Dad sighed. "Tomorrow it'll be over," he said.

Noni felt her stomach jumping around as she herself went to bed early. It was the only thing she could think of to do so that the time would pass and tomorrow would come. She felt like a kid on Christmas Eve, but it was not joyful anticipation that kept her eyes wide open. Was Kip sleepless too? Her parents? Was Bird, who had actually snapped at Kip this evening, asleep? And Neill? Mrs. Balkans? Denise?

No thoughts about Baxly tonight, Noni commanded herself. Thinking about Denise would be the last straw.

She tried to breathe deeply, to relax her muscles by first tightening, then letting them loose. Finally she slid to sleep, but not for long. She kept coming to wakefulness with a jerk, heart beating nervously. Once she woke up in pitch-darkness and heard her parents talking. Mom was saying, "Jim, what will we do if he can't handle it? I can't stand the thought of his failing. I've seen him bloom . . ."

Dad replied, "Dina, don't borrow trouble." But his voice had a scared edge to it, and the sound of it made Noni's tummy tighten as she drifted back to sleep.

She woke a second time, briefly, hearing something bang in the back of her drowsy mind. It was toward dawn, and her room was graying slowly around her. Had someone made a sound? Had Kip fallen out of bed? Noni listened for a moment, then slept again.

This time she dreamed. She dreamed that she

was running the 100-yard dash against Denise again. Denise was ahead of her. Denise had wings growing on her heels, and Mrs. Oliver was standing on the sidelines shouting, "Come on, Denise! Neill admires you so!" Noni's heels were mired in mud. She knew she had to get loose or she'd never, never catch up to Denise, but the sucking mud held her down, imprisoned her feet. Then suddenly the dream shifted, and it was Kip who was stuck in the mud. Kip, who was crying, "Noni, help me . . ."

"No-neeee!"

Had she dreamed that desperate scream? For a confused second, Noni thought she was back on Conan beach, running to help Kip. Then back further in time to the morning when L'il Bird died.

"No-neee! Noni! Noni!"

She sat up, sleep making her dizzy. "What is it? What's happening?" she gasped. From her parents' room she heard sounds. Mom's feet hitting the floor at a run.

"Jim," Mom was crying, "it's Kip . . ."

Kip? Noni was out of her bed, too, running to the door of her room. As she raced down the hall ahead of Mom, she saw Kip's room empty, the bed tumbled and deserted. She heard her name called again.

"He's outside!" Mom urged her. "He's standing by the garage. I saw him from the window."

Noni flew down the stairs, out the open back door. Kip stood barefoot on the cold dewy grass near the garage.

"Bird," he babbled. "Bird, Noni."

She went to him, knelt down beside him, put her arms around him. His sturdy little body was rigid. The look in his eyes scared the wits out of her, but she forced herself to say, "What's wrong, Kip? Tell me!"

Kip's mouth shivered, moved, tried to form words. The only sound that came out was an inhuman, high wail of pain. Noni dropped her arms and forced herself to go over to the garage. As her parents reached Kip, she looked in.

No, she thought. No.

The denim hammock where Bird had sat all these long days had been ripped to shreds. The tangled tape and tubing that had held the bird's legs lay on the floor like dead snakes. The bird itself lay flopped on its side, flapping its wings and yarking with pain and fear.

It couldn't stand up!

It was still crippled. From behind her, Kip's voice rose in a keening howl. Noni covered her ears with her hands, but she couldn't drown out the sounds he made, the sounds of desolation.

Who? she thought wildly. Who did this thing?

14

"Good Lord!" Dad said, behind her.

Noni turned away from the bird, from the ruin of that cantankerous, pampered gull and looked into her father's shocked face.

"I thought I heard a noise out here early this morning, around six," Dad said. "I thought it was some dog or cat nosing around the trash cans. Who'd do something like this?"

"Denise Baxly." The name went off like a firecracker in Noni's head. The creep, she thought. I'll wring her neck!

Dad's eyes were hard as stones, but he said, "We don't know that. You can't go around accusing people without proof."

"Who else would do such a thing? Or want to? Or be mad or mean enough or live near enough—"

"Jim!" Mom called desperately. "Help me!"

She was carrying Kip toward the house, and Dad hurried after them. Noni closed the garage door, not looking at Bird. She couldn't bear to think of Bird right now.

When she got inside the house, Mom was upstairs, trying to soothe Kip.

"Bird!" Kip kept sobbing. "My Bird!" Dad came down the stairs as Noni shut the kitchen door behind her.

"The poor kid," Dad said. Noni noticed Dad's shoulders were hunched over again. "That poor little guy. He loved the bird. If I just knew who did this, I'd . . ."

"What'll you do to Bird?" Noni asked fearfully. She winced when Dad just looked at her in silence. "You're going to . . . to kill it?" she whispered.

"I don't look forward to it, but what else can I do?"

Kip's sobs were getting louder, and Dad headed back upstairs. Noni followed.

"You saw," he said over his shoulder. "The bird's crippled."

"The legs didn't heal. We should have called a vet!" But Denise wouldn't listen. Always, Denise . . .

"Forget about the bird," Dad said roughly. "Let's worry about Kip right now."

Kip . . . and the meet! She had forgotten about it for a minute. "Kip can't . . . Oh, Dad! He'll be able to run?" she gasped.

But Dad didn't hear her. Kip's screams were loud, strident, demanding. Mom had him on the big doubled bed in the master bedroom, and he was drumming his dirty bare feet into the mattress. He rolled his head back and forth on the pillow so that his cries were gasping shrieks.

Noni ran over and dropped on her knees beside Kip. "Kippy, listen, listen to me. Don't work yourself up, please! Today's the day you have to run your race."

He didn't hear her. He couldn't listen. He was running his own race with pain and grief and loss. There was no understanding in Kip's eyes, just horror over what he had seen. Mom looked at Dad.

"We'd better give him some medication," Mom said slowly.

"Medication?" Noni cried. "No—he couldn't run with medication!"

Her parents looked at her.

"Noni . . ." Dad began helplessly.

"Oh, please! Please! Maybe he'll quiet down. Maybe he'll listen to me!" Noni begged. "He worked so hard. We all worked . . ."

"Noni, we don't want to. But we can't let him stay like this."

Dad went to the bathroom and got the medicine Dr. Farrell had prescribed.

"Try to understand," Mom begged.

Noni did understand. She hated Denise Baxly. What wouldn't she do to Baxly, that hateful, spiteful creep! That nasty, slimy, stinking thing! She watched helplessly as Dad shook the brown bottle, poured a teaspoonful and told Mom to steady Kip's head.

Don't drink it! she wanted to cry at Kip. The first spoonful spilled onto the white sheet, as Kip screamed his dirge of pain. "Bird . . . my Bird . . ."

The second spoonful went down, and with it, all of Noni's hopes.

Dad cleared his throat. "The meet isn't for some hours yet," he said. "Maybe the medication will calm him down and wear off by then." Noni knew he was just trying to make her feel better. "Maybe it won't affect his speed."

"It will. You know it will." Noni watched Kip. Mom covered Kip with blankets, held him close, murmured comforting words that did not penetrate his painful cries. She couldn't bear to watch, to see Kip go still and dull, tranquilized beyond pain. She went into her room and sat on her bed, wanting to cry, but again feeling that the tears would not come.

I wanted him to win. I wanted it so bad.

Kip running in the Haymarket meet. Kip with a gleaming gold medal on his chest proudly smiling like those kids in the Special Olympics booklets. Kip racing down state and national track meets, winning them. Kip, the darling of Conan . . .

They were dreams, Noni knew. Just dreams. All that work, all the hope, all the wanting—those were dreams too.

Noni didn't know how long she sat there. In a while, Kip's cries stilled and hushed.

Mom came to her room. "Noni . . ." she began uncertainly. "About the meet today . . ."

Noni looked at Mom dully. She was going to say, now, that Kip couldn't go to the meet. But Mom was saying, "Dad thinks we should go, regardless. I don't want to put Kip through anything like this the way things are, but your father seems to think we should put in an appearance. I wanted to know what you thought."

Noni was beyond thought. "I don't know. It doesn't matter," she said. Mom looked at her worriedly, then left.

"I'll try to call Mrs. Balkans and explain . . ." Her voice drifted away. Noni sat listening, but not really listening, to the telephone being dialed in the now still house. Mrs. Balkans wasn't home. Noni thought, She's gone to Haymarket. She's waiting for Kip.

Apparently Dad had the same thought. "Dina, we have to go. Of course Kip can't race or . . . or do anything. But it would be discourteous not to show up at all after the work everyone's put into training him." He drew a deep breath. "My boss will be down there too, don't forget."

"I know." Mom was close to tears. "I know, Jim. Oh, why did this have to happen? Poor little boy. Poor Noni . . ."

Footsteps, and then Mom again appeared in the doorway of the room. "Noni, get ready. We're going to Haymarket. All right?"

"Kip?" Noni asked, with a small surge of hope. But Mom killed the hope by saying Kip was asleep.

He would be asleep for a while, and then asleep on his feet for hours. He would be disoriented, almost sleepwalking. The stuff Dr. Farrell had given them was pretty potent.

"Noni?" Mom prodded gently.

She nodded, got to her feet and stumbled to her closet. She found jeans, a T-shirt, sneakers. She washed her hands and combed her hair automatically, deliberately not letting herself think about the meet, or of the kids who would be coming to see Conan's darling win, or of the coaches, the well-wishers and . . . Denise Baxly. Especially not of Denise Baxly. Kip's not running was Baxly's victory.

She went downstairs and tried to eat the cereal Mom put in front of her. It stuck in her throat. "I'll get Kip dressed," she told her folks, who nodded without looking at her.

Kip lay like a limp doll on the bed, not offering help or resistance. She got his track things on him, the special shirt with "Conan" printed on it that had been given to the four kids from Conan who were entering the meet, and his new socks and track shoes. He looked up at her, distress and pain buried under layers of medication. How do you feel inside you? Noni wanted to ask. She wanted to put her arms around Kip and hold him. At the same time, she wanted to shake him, scream at him that he had to wake up, to shake off his medication, to win! Win for us! She wanted to cry. We've worked so hard to make you come this far!

"Hey, everyone ready?" The cheerful voice shouting downstairs made Noni's heart stop still. Neill!

She stopped with one sneaker on Kip and one off and ran to the landing to look down the stairs. Neill stood in the hallway, listening as Dad explained what had happened.

"You're kidding!" Neill's face was suddenly pale. "You mean Bird . . . and Kip? Kip's out of it?"

Noni ran down the stairs. She wanted to throw herself into Neill's arms and cry, but she knew if she did that, if she let go now, the tears would never stop coming.

"Bird's out too, Neill. The legs didn't heal."

Neill's voice was hushed. "Is he still there?" he asked. Dad nodded.

"I'll take care of it later. Right now . . ." His voice trailed off.

Neill firmed his young mouth and looked at Noni with a kind of accepting despair. "Noni, it was a fifty-fifty chance," he said. "I guess Bird didn't make it." Noni bit her lip as Neill went on. "You take care of Kip and I . . . and I'll take care of Bird. I'll get my father to help me after you people leave." He looked sick.

Dad looked relieved. Who enjoyed the thought of wringing a gull's neck?

"Are we ready?" Mom asked tightly, and Noni ran back upstairs to get Kip's other sneaker on.

When Kip was finally dressed, Dad drove the car up to the front door and they got in. Neill stood by the window, looking in as Mom and Noni settled Kip in the backseat. Neill looked as if he wanted to say something, but didn't know what to say. What could he say? Noni wondered. Good luck? Have a good day? She grabbed at Neill's hand resting on the car windowsill.

"We were looking forward to Saturday," she managed to say.

His reply was lost in Kip's complaining whimper, and the car started forward. Noni closed her eyes. She hoped Neill would finish Bird off quickly, without pain. She knew that he would bury Bird later, not throw it into the trash like a bunch of garbage.

Don't think that way! she told herself. As they drove toward Haymarket, she tried not to remember how happy they had been just last Monday, how everything seemed to be going their way. How quickly things changed, Noni thought.

Well, she'd change things for Denise too—that was one thing for sure. Hating made Noni feel better. Hating was better than grieving. She'd fix it so that Baxly would never be able to hold her head up again in Conan. She'd get her in school, confront her, tell her that she never thought anyone could be so inhuman as to destroy a little boy's dream.

It was quiet in the car, and the sudden sound of the radio made Noni jump. Dad had just turned it on. The radio announcer's voice was saying ". . . an item of local interest: Large crowds are gathering at Haymarket High today.

It's the annual Haymarket Special Olympics meet held for very special athletes. We at station KBZ wish all the Olympians and all the hardworking people who have made today possible the best of luck, on this glorious spring day . . ."

Click. Dad shut off the radio. They reached Haymarket in silence.

It was hard to find a parking space. As the radio announcer had said, a lot of people were at the Haymarket High School field. "Olympian?" a policeman asked, stopping them, and seeing Kip, pointed a finger toward a parking lot. "Reserved for contestants." His voice was warm. "Good luck."

"Thank you," Dad said. Mom said nothing and neither did Noni. Kip moved his head and murmured dreamily.

Dad maneuvered the car into a parking spot. They should have all gotten out of the car, but they sat there. "We're here," Dad finally said.

Mom stirred, as if to speak. Noni knew that Mom was going to beg Dad to turn the car around and drive back to Conan. Who could blame her? But—

"He has to try," Noni whispered. "He came all this way."

Dad drew a deep breath. "Dina," he said, ignoring Noni, "if you want, we'll go home." He spoke gently, and Noni saw him reach out to cup Mom's face in his big hands. She could almost hear the sound of her parents' hearts breaking. "Whatever you say, Dina. I'll do what you want me to do."

She held her breath. Then Mom said, "Noni's right. He's come all this way. Kip has to at least

. . . show. We can't take him back to hide him."

"Right," Dad said, without any joy, without any kind of feeling. He got out of the car and started to help Kip out.

"Noni!" It was Mrs. Balkans, hurrying over to them. "My goodness, you people took your time getting here. We were starting to worry . . ." She saw Kip, and her hand flew to her mouth. "What happened?"

Dad explained. "Oh, no!" Mrs. Balkans groaned. "Is there some way of snapping him out of this? Walking him around, maybe—"

"It wouldn't do any good." Mom took Kip's limp hand in hers. "We only brought him because we knew you'd be waiting, Mrs. Balkans. Kip couldn't even walk a straight line right now."

Mrs. Balkans looked ready to cry. "How terrible! And he was sure to win!" Then she rallied. "You know, in Special Olympics, medication *is* allowed, unlike in normal athletic meets. Perhaps by the time Kip's 50-yard dash is announced, he'll feel more himself. In the meantime he can march in the parade. All the Olympians are going to march in the parade. He shouldn't have to miss that."

Mom and Dad looked at each other. "What harm could it do?"

Kip was walked away between Dad and Mom, with Mrs. Balkans following. Noni wanted to stay where she was, but her coach said, "Coming, Noni?" Noni's unwilling feet dragged her forward.

She knew she had to finish what she had begun.

15

It was a beautiful day. Gold sun, blue sky as clear as it could be. Sometimes a gentle breeze tugged at the flags that decorated Haymarket High School, or rippled across the tops of the stands that dotted the sidelines. Neill and the other boys from Conan Junior High had helped make some of those stands. One sold hot dogs, ice cream, and soft drinks . . . another, souvenirs, pennants, candy. She passed a stand and saw a glitter of medals, bronze and silver and gold, and her heart caught and tugged like a raw nerve ending.

Kip should have owned one of those by tonight, she thought, again fighting the urge to run back to the car and lock herself in with her disappointment.

"Noni!" Brenda was running up, waving, urgent and flushed. "Mrs. Balkans needs you. We're getting the Conan kids lined up for the big parade." Noni nodded, glad to be able to do something, wishing that Brenda wouldn't say anything about Kip. But, "I nearly died when I heard about Kip," Brenda went on as they walked toward a corner of the field where a large group of people and Special Olympians had gathered. "It's so awful!

You must feel terrible, Noni. All our work gone up in smoke. What happened?"

Noni almost told Brenda about the gull and about Denise. But now wasn't the time. Time to hate Baxly afterward, cut her name to ribbons so that she couldn't look anybody in the eye again! Right now they had a parade to get under way.

Haymarket High School had gotten together an honor guard of high school students, the high school band, and more Haymarket kids who carried banners for the Special Olympics, for Haymarket High, the state flag, and the Stars and Stripes. They had done this to honor the Olympians, but the contrast between the tall, straight-limbed boys and girls and the athletes was poignantly obvious. Noni's hands became tight fists as she saw Kip and Georgie McKenna shambling along beside their briskly marching honor guard. Kip didn't even know where he was. Nearly all the other athletes were smiling, but their bodies wouldn't always obey them. There was a little kid on crutches, an older girl in a wheelchair, a gently smiling adult who waved at everyone. Some of the athletes had to be guided by coaches who walked beside them.

"Sad," Noni heard someone murmur beside her. "Poor things!"

She hadn't wanted pity for Kip. No way! You gave pity to losers.

Noni looked away from the parade, finding Mrs. McKenna standing in a booth nearby. With her was an elderly man, the mayor of the city of Lincoln, someone said. Milling around the stand were several volunteers. Referees, assistant coaches, a few sports celebrities who had been asked to come and give a few hours of time in "clinics" during the meet. There were also teen-agers who had volunteered to act as "hug-gers"—kids who encouraged and hugged every Special Olympian after every event. This was one of the ways in which every athlete was made to feel happy and proud, whether the event was won or lost.

Noni's eyes roved on, looking for her parents. Dad had taken Mom away from the crowded seats that ringed one side of the track. He had led her to a spot some distance away, and he had an arm around her. Mom's face was pressed against Dad's shoulder. Noni wished she were little enough to run to them and feel their comforting arms around her.

It took an effort for Noni to keep her face calm and still while the mayor made a speech about the aims of the Special Olympics. He honored, he said, the efforts of the volunteers, and the cour-age, the determination of the athletes. "Everyone here is a winner," the mayor said, and Noni wanted to laugh bitterly. What did the mayor know about losing? Kip's kind of losing? Get out of there, Noni wanted to shout at the mayor.

Then Mrs. McKenna made a much shorter speech, and the athletes repeated the words used at every Special Olympics meet. This made Noni want to cry, especially that part about "being brave in the attempt." Kip's attempt would have been so brave! It would have succeeded!

Someone was punching her arm. "Noni, wake up! Mrs. Balkans wants us over there with the Conan kids. They're announcing the softball throw."

Noni joined Mrs. Balkans and Mr. Crusoe and the other kids who had worked with the Conan athletes. She tried to feel some enthusiasm as one of the little girls from Conan made a good throw, and was congratulated not just by her "hugger" but by the other kids who had competed against her.

"Now, that's the spirit of this meet," Mrs. Balkans said proudly, but Noni found no such spirit in herself. She was glad when Dad came over to her a while later.

"I think it's time to go," he said. "We've made our appearance. This whole thing's murder on your mother." He paused. "Get Kip, and let's go."

Noni turned to find Kip. She had assumed he was standing where she had last seen him, among the kids from Conan. When he wasn't there, she was irritated. Where could he have got to? Disoriented by the tranquilizer, he had probably gone off in search of Mom and Dad. She looked around but couldn't spot him.

Dad frowned when she told him she couldn't find Kip. "I thought you were keeping an eye on him!" he snapped. "Ask Mrs. Balkans. Maybe she knows."

Noni saw Mrs. Balkans' red hair waving like a flag in the midst of the crowd. When she reached the coach, Mrs. Balkans was doing warm-ups with the Conan special athletes. She stopped at the sight of Noni.

"What's wrong? . . . Kip? . . . No, come to think of it, I haven't seen him for a while. Ask Mr. Crusoe."

Noni began to worry a little as Mr. Crusoe examined the boys' bathrooms and found no one.

"All this noise and cheering—maybe Kip got scared and went to the car," he told her.

Noni nodded, keeping her eyes low, concentrating on the sparkle of Mr. Crusoe's referee's whistle that hung around his neck. If she looked into Mr. Crusoe's face, she was afraid she would see her own rising panic mirrored in his eyes. "It's not like him to wander off like this," she muttered.

Mr. Crusoe went with her to the parking lot. There was no Kip. By now Noni was really scared. While Mr. Crusoe alerted the policeman in the parking lot, she raced back to the field. Maybe Kip had been found. Please, she thought. Please . . .

No one had found Kip. She could see Dad walking up and down around the stands, while Mom hurried farther downfield, looking too. Kip had dropped out of sight. How? Where? Noni made her way back to Mrs. Balkans.

The coach was very upset. "As if things weren't bad enough, poor little guy!" She stopped to add, "Come to think of it, he was standing right next to me when I told Jean McKenna we had to take him out of the 50-yard dash. I didn't think he could possibly understand me, what with the tranquilizer and all, but do you think that upset him? Maybe he ran off someplace because of that?"

Kip hiding someplace. Kip cowering in an alleyway after running away from that hated school in Lincoln. Noni remembered what Aunt Mary had said about Kip not being able to cope with a race.

"Don't worry, Noni," Mrs. Balkans was soothing. "There are a hundred places he could have got to." Noni started to answer, but just then the loudspeaker began to announce the 50-yard dash.

She had waited so long for this moment to come, and now it meant nothing. Worse than nothing. Where *was* Kip? She turned eagerly as she saw Mr. Crusoe jogging back from the parking lot, and slumped again when she saw that he was alone and shaking his head.

"Where—" she began and then stopped right there. She had just seen Kip!

Mrs. Balkans saw him at the same time. "What in the world—" she began and stopped, grabbing Noni's arm.

The contestants for the 50-yard dash were filing onto the field. Kip was among them. He was lining up as he had been taught to do, for his race—his big race!

Noni felt relief tumble into another kind of panic for him. "Mrs. Balkans, he shouldn't be up there! He doesn't even know what's happening! He couldn't even walk a straight line right now."

Mrs. Balkans was already hurrying forward, but the referee saw her and gently waved her back. "Only contestants are allowed past the starting line," he said. "No coaches!"

"Get him out of there!" It was Dad, standing right behind Noni. "If you don't do something, Mrs. Balkans, I will!"

"Wait." The coach put her hand on Dad's arm. The referee's voice, telling the 50-yard-dash runners what to do, floated down to them.

"You all understand what happens now, right? Everyone ready . . ."

The runners went down. Noni's mouth felt dry. "I have to get him out!" Dad muttered.

"Not now. If you go over there now, it'll be worse for him than if you just let him run," Mrs. Balkans argued.

"Set . . ."

Little heads went up, poised and ready—all but

Kip's. Kip was in a world of his own. Noni's muscles bunched with readiness. She wanted so much to run for Kip. She found herself praying for a miracle. Maybe the drug had worn off. Maybe Kip's feet would be swift.

BANG! The starting pistol cracked. They were off.

Everyone, that is, except Kip.

Kip stood at the starting line, dazed, still crouched. Dad groaned, and Noni stared horrified, seeing her nightmare come true. Kip was mired to the ground. Slowly he began to straighten out. Noni heard Brenda's voice crying, "Kip . . . come *on!*"

One of the runners broke through the finish tape, was hugged jubilantly. Another child followed. Kip still stood at the starting line, swaying, staring at the ground.

"I'm going for him," Dad said through gritted teeth. "He doesn't even know where he is."

Noni turned away, unable to look. Would Kip scream and cry when Dad took him and led him away?

Then Mrs. Balkans gasped, "Oh, . . ." She grabbed Noni's arm, pinching hard. "Look!"

Noni turned and saw that Kip had started to run. He ran as if he were in a dream, fighting against fog. Foot up, foot down, arm in, arm out. A gentle, sighing sound rippled through the crowd.

Surely Kip knew the race was over? Noni ached for him. Ten yards . . . fifteen. Then he stumbled, fell painfully, banging his knees on the hard track. A cry tore from Noni's mouth, and was echoed by those around her "Kip . . .

come on!" Noni cried out. The crowd picked it up.

"Come on, Kip! Get up, guy! Come on!"

Kip slowly got up and started moving forward again. He was limping, but Noni could sense his determination. He was going to finish this race, not for the sake of winning a medal, but because he would not quit. Prickles ran up and down Noni's arms as she watched Kip's small figure shambling forward, for she knew the effort he was making. Around her, the cheers of the crowd had become shouts of encouragement.

"Come on, champ!" a man's voice cried, and Noni saw Mr. Crusoe standing by the finish line, holding out his arms to Kip. "You'll make it, Kip."

Kip's feet inched over the finish line.

"A winner!" a woman said. "A real winner . . ." and there was no pity for Kip anymore, only admiration and joy.

Noni felt tears drench her face as she repeated, "A winner."

Dad was racing away from Noni, toward Kip. Mom had already reached him. Mrs. Balkans was there too. As Noni watched, everyone hugged Kip, and Mr. Crusoe solemnly pulled his referee's whistle from around his neck and draped it around Kip's neck.

The crowd went wild. "Yea, Kip!" they screamed and shouted, clapping and whooping. Noni glimpsed the mayor of Lincoln. Tears were streaming down his cheeks.

"Noni . . . hey, Noni! How about that? Kip didn't let us down!" That was Brenda, on her way to Kip. Noni started to follow, then stopped. What do you mean, she wanted to cry out, Kip didn't let *us* down? Kip didn't run that race for *us*.

And then Denise Baxly's words came back. *I thought you wanted to do something for Kip, but you're a hypocrite. You did this for yourself!*

That wasn't true—no way! Yet Noni's mind was racing. So many good things had happened to her because she tried to get Kip into the Haymarket race. There was her popularity in school—even Neill liking her. Her parents' pride in her. Conan talking about her. She had started by wanting to win this race for Kip and had ended by wanting the glory for herself. Using Kip . . .

She felt sick.

How could she go and hug Kip now? She felt mean and small and petty. She turned to run away from the crowd and jubilation, but Dad's voice stopped her.

"Noni! Where are you going?"

He caught her as she tried to stumble away. His face shone with pride, but then he didn't realize what she had done. A huge sob exploded out of her, and she found herself burrowing into Dad's arms.

"It's over," Dad said, misunderstanding. "Kip's a winner, just as you always knew he'd be."

"But I didn't know. I nearly messed it all up!" she wailed, knowing she had to tell someone, even though Dad would hate and loathe her. Straining, tumbling, her words came out. "I wanted to be popular. I wanted people to look up to me. When Kip couldn't run this morning I thought, How could he let *me* down? Selfish, thinking of myself . . ."

Dad held her while she sobbed. How could he bear to touch her? Noni didn't know, because she couldn't stand herself. But even when she'd cried herself out, Dad didn't let her go. Then he pushed her away a little, to look down into her tear-blotched face.

"Noni," he said, and his voice was gentle, "I guess you're kind of human after all and not the ministering angel people were starting to make you out to be. I have to say it's a relief." He smiled at her, his big knuckles wiping away the tears. "Girl, all of us want to be proud of the ones we love. Sometimes our pride gets away from us. That's normal. Sometimes, pride turns to bitterness . . ."

He wasn't just talking about her, Noni knew. His voice, his eyes brought back memories of bitter fights and angry times. "Noni, all I can say to you is that we've all of us come a ways together. Families travel together and grow, just as individuals do. I know Kip has grown, for one thing. It took a lot for him to finish that hopeless race in front of all these people. You gave him confidence and belief in himself and physical ability to make that effort, Noni. You should be proud."

"But I . . ."

"Know why you should be proud? Because you made it possible for Kip to give *us* something today. Think of that, Noni. Because of you, Kip gave us today, which we'll never forget." Dad loosened her. "Wipe your eyes, now, honey. The champ's asking for his Noni."

Noni watched Dad walk away. Inside her, the stone-cold grief was melting and small jumps of happiness had begun. She felt as she had felt the day she learned Neill liked her—excited, a little scared. *Kip gave us today*, she thought and held the thought close to her. It pulsated, warm and gentle, like a second heart.

"Noni. Noni!" It was Neill's voice, close behind her.

She turned quickly, saw him galloping up toward her.

"Man," he panted. "That was some race! Dad and I, we barely got to see it. We just drove in a minute ago. Kip is something!"

Noni felt joy swoop through her. "Isn't he? Isn't he great?"

Neill nodded. "We were sure he wouldn't be able to run. That's why Mom and Eddie didn't come with us. But I knew you'd want to know about Bird, so I asked Dad to drive me over right away."

"Neill, not now!" She didn't want to think of sad things right then.

He grabbed her hands. "Listen, will you? Bird is all right!" She stared at him. "I mean it! He's walking around under Mom's laundry basket. He tried to escape from the garage, see, and she . . ."

"Walking? Neill Oliver, that's impossible! I saw him this morning as limp as a rag doll. His legs were still broken."

Neill gave her a superior look. "If you were in traction, had been for months, and the cast suddenly came off, I'll bet you'd feel great, wouldn't you? I'll bet you could run the 100-yard dash?"

"Get to the point!" she hollered at him.

"The point is that Bird needed some time to get the blood circulating in his legs before he could stand up! He was flopping around because it was too soon. You should see him now. He thinks he's God gift to the bird world—mean and real nasty!"

Noni began to laugh in sheer relief and joy. She

wanted to turn cartwheels, sing, cry, shout with happiness. She threw her arms around Neill and hugged him. "Whoopee!" she yelled, and he laughed while they both hollered, "Hooray!"

Oh, the world was beautiful. It was a wonderful place!

16

Now it was Saturday night.

The long, gold-and-blue day had ended, even though Noni had wanted, several times, to shout, "Stop!" One of the times when she wanted time to hold still was when Kip put his arms around her, saying, "Noni, Noni, Kip happy."

Another time was when Kip saw Bird again, after they got back to Conan. The look on Kip's face when he saw mean old Bird on his feet, and Kip's joyous cry, had made them all choke up. Then, there was the celebration at the Harlow home, with everyone dropping in—Mr. Crusoe, Mrs. Balkans, Dad's boss, teachers and kids and neighbors. So many people, all wishing Kip well.

The Baxlys came by, minus Denise. Mrs. Baxly said Denise had a headache and was lying down. Sure, Noni thought, sure she has a headache! Her rotten scheme backfired. That's why she has a headache.

She hadn't thought of Denise during the day. To think of her would have spoiled things she didn't want spoiled. If she couldn't bottle time and hoard the good moments, she wanted the day at least free of Baxly.

But now, with the day's ending, she needed to think of Denise and what to do about her.

Noni stood in her room, getting ready for her date with Neill. It was a shame, she thought, that her first date, her big moment, was being partially spoiled because of Baxly. Spoiled it was, because no matter how she tried, she kept thinking of how Bird had looked this morning, and Kip's desolation. She tried to tell herself that Monday was time enough to deal with her enemy, but she knew that if she didn't get things squared away tonight, have it all out in the open, she wouldn't enjoy the movie or Neill's company.

"Noni, are you getting ready?" Mom called.

Noni glanced at her watch. There was time to see Denise if she wanted to. The question was, Did she want to?

She looked out her bedroom window into the street below and across to where many lights shone from the Baxly house. There were no cars parked in the driveway, though, and Noni guessed that Denise's parents were out. Denise would be there alone.

She left the window and went downstairs, to where Dad smiled at her over the top of the newspaper. In the kitchen Noni could hear Mom phoning Aunt Mary, telling her how the mayor of Lincoln had called Kip "an example of the Special Olympics spirit." Kip himself was humming a happy song, somewhere. Everyone's happy, Noni thought, but me. I have to go and have it out with Baxly. Now.

She felt jumpy. She couldn't even return Dad's smile properly. "I'm going for a walk," she told him. "Be right back."

She slipped out the door and walked down the quiet sidewalk. It wasn't cold, but there was a coldness in her, and she hugged her arms tightly to her as she stopped in front of the Baxly house. She hesitated, and then saw, in her mind's eye, Denise sneaking down the sidewalk, creeping into the garage, tearing Bird out of his hammock . . .

Noni knocked on the door. She waited, but there was no answer. She knocked again. Finally the door opened.

Denise's eyes were red, and she kept her hands behind her back. "What do you want?" she demanded in a surly voice.

Noni had prepared a speech damning Denise, but now it left her mind. "Why?" she demanded. "Just tell me, why did you do it?"

"I don't know what you're talking about," Denise said coldly.

"Yes, you do! You're not just a sneaking creep, but a lying coward too. You tried to hurt Bird to spite me and to make sure Kip got so worked up he wouldn't win the race. Now I want to know how even you could have thought up such a rotten trick!"

Silence. Denise didn't deny a word of what Noni had said. She started to close the door, but Noni hurled herself against it, pushing Denise backward into the house. "Show me your hands!" she shouted. "Bird hurt you, didn't he? Good for him! Show me. Why did you want to hurt a poor innocent gull? And Kip—what did he ever do to you?"

Denise said thickly, "I didn't mean to hurt the bird. I thought he'd be okay. Ma kept saying wild animals shouldn't be kept as pets, and she said Bird's legs should be healed by now. I just wanted to let him loose and shake you up. I didn't think he'd be . . . crippled." She turned away from Noni. "I didn't want your brother out of the race, either. How'd I know he'd react like that?"

Her voice shook, but Noni felt no pity. "You wanted to hurt me, didn't you? Admit it!"

"Why not?" Denise sounded dull, uncaring. "You were so high and mighty. The great Noni Harlow. You acted like—like Ma does, you know that?"

"Like your *mother?*" Noni was nearly speechless.

"She likes to take the credit for things. She's always after me to win, be the best, be the first." Denise's voice was a bitter murmur. "She wants to have me number one because then she's number one. She sure didn't let me forget it when you got so important because of Kip. She kept asking me why I hadn't thought of such a simple thing as helping to train a retarded child."

Noni winced, not at the words, but at the pain in Denise's voice. Denise in pain? The great Baxly hurt?

"She won't tolerate failure," Denise continued. "Do you know what she told me when you won the 100-yard dash? She told me she can't stand losers. 'I cannot abide a loser,'" Denise mimicked harshly.

Noni could hear Mrs. Baxly saying that. She wanted to say something, but no words came.

"Dad's like that too. So am I, don't misunderstand me. I like to win." Denise's chin went up and Noni's pity dissolved as she saw the old Denise, the one she had envied and disliked. "But then . . . I saw what you were doing for Kip. You were doing it because you wanted something good for him, not for yourself. I admired you for that and I—I wanted to try to help you." Denise's voice rose angrily. "I did help you."

"Really? Is that why you laughed at Marcie's crummy joke about Kip?" Denise was silent. "Why, if you wanted to help me?"

Denise didn't really answer that question. "Marcie . . . and Brenda," she said thoughtfully. "I thought they were my friends, but they weren't. I guess maybe I didn't have any friends. They all just hung around me because that was a cool thing to do. Then it got to be cool to hang around you." Again her voice hardened. "You had it all. You had friends. You were a good runner. And Neill always liked you."

Her voice cracked suddenly, and she became still. Noni thought confusedly, she sounds lonely. She didn't want to see this part of Denise. It made Denise too human, too hard to hate. Why was Denise jealous of me? Noni wondered. She had so much.

In spite of herself, Noni seemed to be looking into Denise and feeling how it must be to live with the constant demand of perfection. To be the best, to be number one—not just in sports, at school, but with boys, friends, and at home. Especially at home. No slouching for Denise, Noni knew, because her parents kept demanding one more ribbon, another victory, another "first." Noni recalled what Dad had said to her today about growing, about Kip "giving them today." The Baxlys would never have seen Kip's performance that way. Noni shuddered.

Denise has always been lonely, she thought. Lonelier than I ever have been! The discovery shook her.

By now Denise had regained her composure.

"What'll you do in school? Blab about Bird?" she asked, her eyes glinting. "I'll deny it was me, you know. It won't be easy, convincing people. You think you have friends now, but wait. They'll come flocking back the second you trip up, make a mistake, stop being so 'in'! As soon as they forget about Kip, they'll forget you too."

Marcie would do that, maybe Brenda too. But Noni didn't care about friends like that. She meant to tell Denise that she would tell everyone in school, but the words came out differently.

"Bird's okay," she said.

"What do you mean—okay?"

Noni found herself explaining. "He's at the Olivers', right now. In a few days we'll be able to take him to the wildlife sanctuary at Martha's Vineyard and set him free. Kip may take it hard, but I think he'll understand." Her voice filled with pride as she added, "Kip understands a lot these days. He's pretty sharp."

Denise didn't say anything, but her eyes suddenly filled. As Noni stared, slow tears began to roll down her cheeks. "I'm glad he's okay," she whispered. "I . . . I'm so glad."

Suddenly she was sobbing, leaning up against the door, with her scratched fingers covering her cheeks. Noni felt embarrassed to see Baxly cry. Embarrassed and . . . touched? How could she be touched by this enemy?

Mom was calling Noni's name. She had to go. She would be late for that show if she didn't go. Yet Noni lingered, unsatisfied, confused, wanting to say something to Denise. What to say? The words wouldn't come. Maybe there weren't any right words.

"I'll see you at school," she finally said. "And

. . . I won't tell anyone. There's no point. Kip got what he wanted, and the bird's okay."

Denise didn't answer her, but held open the door of the house. Noni went through the open door and stopped on the steps, uncertain, as the door shut behind her.

What to do now? Was Denise still crying behind the door? Should she knock on the door again? And then what?

Noni slowly climbed down the front steps. She shouldn't be thinking of Denise anymore. She wasn't going to tell on her at school. Wasn't that enough? They were quits. Denise *had* helped with Kip, now Noni was helping her with silence.

And yet . . .

We almost talked today, she thought. We nearly talked about friends who weren't real friends, and jealousy and loneliness and . . . growing. Did friendships grow? Noni wondered, and then had to stop in her tracks to think that one out.

She had tried being friends with Baxly before, and it hadn't worked. It had been a disaster.

Noni looked over her shoulder. The Baxly house was quiet now, and dark, except for the light in the living room. Noni saw that Denise hadn't closed the door all the way. A tiny sliver of light shone through the crack in the door.

It was just a little light, but the glow lit Noni all the way home, to where Neill was waiting.

ABOUT THE AUTHOR

MAUREEN CRANE WARTSKI was born in Ashiya, Japan, and lived there until she was seventeen. She attended the University of Redlands in California, and Sophia University in Tokyo. She has visited many countries around the world, and lived in Bangkok, Thailand, for five years.

A writer since she sold her first story at age fourteen, she has been an English teacher both overseas and in this country. In her spare time she enjoys silk-screen printing, gardening, and sailing near her home in Sharon, Massachusetts, where she lives with her husband, Mike, their sons Bert and Mark, a sleepy cat, and a cowardly collie named Brandy. The cat and Brandy often share their home with temporary guests, such as orphaned baby squirrels and a crippled black duck that became the model for Bird in the book.